O9-ABF-849

He had a sudden conviction that she was afraid. Not afraid of the burglars, but of him.

"Laurel, I thought the car burglary at the hospital last week was a random thing, but now your new apartment is broken into. Nothing was taken either time. That's very odd."

She wouldn't meet his gaze. "I don't have anything valuable."

"Apparently someone thinks you do."

Her mouth went stiff, and she said nothing. Dan considered pressing the issue. He was walking a fine line between helping a woman he cared about and rooting out the truth. What did he really know about her, after all? Next to nothing.

He didn't want to break her trust, to drive her away, but he couldn't let that cloud his judgment, especially as a police officer. Laurel was an enigma, always on guard.

Maybe she had good reason.

SUSAN PAGE DAVIS

is a native of central Maine. She and her husband, Jim, have six children and five grandchildren. Susan has many years of experience as a freelancer for a daily newspaper. Her books include eight historical novels, two children's books and several romantic suspense novels. With her daughter, Megan, she writes cozy mysteries. Visit Susan's Web site at: www.susanpagedavis.com.

SUSAN PAGE DAVIS
Just Cause

Steeple Hill®

Published by Steeple Hill Books™

If you purchased this book without a cover you should be aware that this book is stolen property. It was reported as "unsold and destroyed" to the publisher, and neither the author nor the publisher has received any payment for this "stripped book."

STEEPLE HILL BOOKS

Steeple
Hill®

ISBN-13: 978-0-373-44276-8
ISBN-10:   0-373-44276-9

JUST CAUSE

Copyright © 2008 by Susan Page Davis

All rights reserved. Except for use in any review, the reproduction or utilization of this work in whole or in part in any form by any electronic, mechanical or other means, now known or hereafter invented, including xerography, photocopying and recording, or in any information storage or retrieval system, is forbidden without the written permission of the editorial office, Steeple Hill Books, 233 Broadway, New York, NY 10279 U.S.A.

This is a work of fiction. Names, characters, places and incidents are either the product of the author's imagination or are used fictitiously, and any resemblance to actual persons, living or dead, business establishments, events or locales is entirely coincidental.

This edition published by arrangement with Steeple Hill Books.

® and TM are trademarks of Steeple Hill Books, used under license. Trademarks indicated with ® are registered in the United States Patent and Trademark Office, the Canadian Trade Marks Office and in other countries.

www.SteepleHill.com

Printed in U.S.A.

But the salvation of the righteous is of the Lord;
He is their strength in the time of trouble.
—*Psalms* 37:39

To my lovely and brilliant critique partners,
Darlene Franklin, Vickie McDonough,
Lynette Sowell and Lisa Harris. Thank you
for your input on this and other books. You each
have your own strengths, and I am blessed
to have you for first readers.

Acknowledgments

Two Maine trial attorneys helped me in portraying
Laurel's situation, the courtroom scenes and pretrial
activity for this book. I'd like to thank Dan Dubord
and John Youney for the pointers they gave me. Any
mistakes or unrealistic representations of the legal
process are entirely my fault.

PROLOGUE

Laurel Hatcher trudged down the long hallway behind the prison guard, her pulse hammering. When she stepped into the interview room, her lawyer, Jim Hight, was already seated at the center table with his briefcase open.

"Hi, Laurel, how are you doing?" He rose to his full six-foot-two-inch height and remained standing until she was seated.

She slid into the chair opposite him. The guard closed the door and waited outside.

Laurel swallowed hard. "I'm okay."

"You sure?"

She nodded. Jim wasn't one to encourage emotional scenes, but he always showed concern for her. Of course, it was business, but she felt there was some sort of respect between them. The last few weeks had splintered her courage and her self-respect, however, and she knew she couldn't stay calm much longer.

"Just get me out of here." Her voice shook, and she clutched the edge of the table.

"We've been granted another bail hearing tomorrow morning."

She inhaled deeply, trying not to let the hope take root. "Do I get real clothes?"

"Not yet."

Laurel wrinkled her nose.

"It's all right to show a little emotion during the hearing," Jim said. "Let the judge see that you cared about your husband. We don't want a major rainstorm in the courtroom, but a few tears would be appropriate."

"I'll see what I can do."

He flashed her a brief, cynical smile. "I know this is tough, but the court has to see the real you tomorrow, not the crusty shell you've built up over the past few weeks."

She exhaled. Could she stay tough for one more day inside the county jail, then suddenly become soft and vulnerable again when she stepped into the courtroom, ready to expose her shredded nerves to strangers?

"I'll try."

"Good. We've got Judge Elliott, which is in our favor, but it'll be tough to get any judge to grant bail in a capital case. I think I can convince him that you're not a flight risk. We'll see what happens."

"What about the evidence?" she asked.

"This is about your character. You have no prior record, and you've always been honest and dependable."

"But the district attorney will try to keep me in here until the trial."

"It's standard in this type of case, and your in-laws are putting some pressure on him," Jim admitted.

"Do you really think we have a chance?" The fear began to rise inside her again.

He sighed. "You've got to keep a positive outlook."

"They turned us down the first time you asked for bail, and I've spent the last five weeks in jail." Her voice cracked a little, and tears stung her eyes. She blinked and looked away. She didn't need to hear him tell her to save her tears for the jury.

As he watched her, her doubts grew. He was a small-town lawyer. She should have hired someone more dynamic, a powerhouse attorney with a proven track record on homicide cases. But with her assets tied up, that was impossible.

"What happens if they release me?"

He sat back and studied her face. "We'll find a place for you to stay until the trial."

"And if the judge refuses to let me out?"

He winced. "You've got to be prepared for that. I'm sorry... It will mean another eight to twelve months in here, I'm guessing."

There ought to be more he could do. Why didn't he assure her that they would win? Shouldn't he be going over the prosecutor's case and pointing out to her all the gaps in it? *I could be in here for the rest of my life!*

"So you're not optimistic about this hearing."

"Not really." His eyes didn't quite meet hers.

"And for the trial?"

He hesitated, and her heart sank.

"I'm doing everything I can to build up a defense that will counteract anything the prosecution can bring on."

"They have no proof."

"I know, but there is some circumstantial evidence." He shrugged. "We should be all right."

Should be. She pulled in a ragged breath. "If they

convict me, I won't win the civil suit. I won't be able to pay you."

"Well, we both knew that at the outset, didn't we?"

She looked at him long and hard, wanting to believe he was doing everything possible. He met her gaze, honest regret reflected in his dark eyes. He wasn't hiding anything.

She stood on shaky legs.

"Laurel, wash your hair tonight."

His request raised her hackles, and she glared at him.

He smiled gently. "I'm not trying to insult you. Just be squeaky-clean and fluff your hair out around your face, okay? No braids tomorrow. We want a soft, vulnerable look."

She felt anxious for their meeting to end.

"I put some money in your account here," he said.

"How much?"

"Fifty. Is that enough? If you need more…"

"It's plenty."

He nodded. "All right. Tell me if you need more later. I'll see you at the courthouse."

"Sure. I'll be there in my basic orange."

She turned toward the door and heard his chair scrape on the concrete floor.

"Laurel, don't go to pieces on me."

He knew her better than she'd realized. She didn't answer but walked toward the door.

"Look, if you stay awake all night, you'll be haggard and ugly in the morning."

She turned and glowered at him. "Thanks. I really needed that."

"I'm sorry." He looked at her sympathetically. "But you need the judge's sympathy, and you need to hold it together. Don't come to court with raccoon eyes."

"Why don't you just send a stylist to my cell in the morning?"

She knocked on the door, and the guard opened it. Remorse hit her halfway down the hall. Jim was just trying to do his job…and he was right. A judge wouldn't look favorably on a bitter, defiant woman.

As her cell door closed behind her ten minutes later, Laurel walked unsteadily to her cot and sat down. Renee was sprawled on her cot across the small room, flipping through a tabloid magazine. Beside her lay the packet of candy Laurel had ordered a week ago.

"That your lawyer again?" Renee's dark eyes glinted.

"Yeah."

"He bring you any money?"

Reluctantly, Laurel nodded.

Renee grinned. "How much?"

"Just tell me what you want, and I'll order it."

Renee's eyes went steely. "I said, how much?"

"Fifty."

"Is that all?"

"Yes." Laurel lay down against the thin pillow.

Renee unwrapped a small piece of candy and popped it into her mouth. "Maybe you should just tell that hotshot lawyer to put something in my account."

"He wouldn't do that."

The candy wrapper crinkled as Renee rolled it between her fingers. "I bet he would if he thought it would help you stay healthy."

Laurel rolled over and faced the wall.

"Did he get you another bail hearing?"

"Tomorrow." The tears were unstoppable now. Laurel burrowed her face into her pillow.

"What's your problem?" Renee snorted. "This could be your last night in the clink, and you're bawling like a baby. It's almost as if you want to stay here."

Laurel shuddered. *Oh, God, help me. Don't leave me in here.* She wiped her face with her sleeve, determined to stop the tears. *Dear Lord, if you're still there...* She had to believe God was real, and that He was watching over her. If He was, then He knew what she needed. And if somehow all her life she'd gotten it wrong, and He wasn't there in her absolute blackest moment, then it didn't matter that she couldn't find the words.

Renee's cot creaked, and the pages of the tabloid rustled. Laurel took a deep breath and stared at the concrete wall. When her cellmate spoke again, Laurel jumped. Renee was close to her, bending down to speak in a loud whisper. "If you do beat this murder rap and get out of here, don't forget your friends."

A piece of candy landed on the blanket near Laurel's hand. She clenched her teeth to hold back a sob.

ONE

Two years later

"I'm sorry, but we can't offer you the position. I'm sure you understand." The interviewer eyed Laurel over the top of her glasses.

. Laurel breathed deeply to control her disappointment. She understood, all right. The hospital couldn't have someone like her on the front desk, meeting the public. The question "Have you ever been arrested?" always wrecked it for her.

"We have a part-time evening position, however," the hospital's personnel director said. "You seem to be qualified to maintain our Web site…"

Laurel hesitated. "I might be able to do that."

The woman handed her a sheet of paper. "Why don't you look this over. If you're interested, call me tomorrow before five."

Laurel folded the paper. "Thank you." It was better than a stark dismissal, but not much. Twenty hours or so a week, at minimum wage.

The sun was sinking as she climbed the concrete steps to the upper level of the hospital's outdoor parking lot. She passed a group of visitors approaching the building and averted her eyes.

She'd been in Ohio for two weeks and had been turned down for more than a dozen jobs. She supposed she ought to take this one, although she'd never used her computer skills professionally, and it wasn't the type of job she would have chosen. Her funds were dwindling fast. The trip, the deposit on her modest apartment, groceries… She'd had the phone connected right away—court's orders. If she didn't find some income soon, she wouldn't have enough money to stay afloat.

She glanced ahead toward her dark green Toyota Camry and caught her breath. A ruggedly built man was opening the driver's-side door.

She wanted to call out, but fear silenced her and she clutched the railing.

They found me! Somehow, they found me, and they're going to send me back to prison.

But that was irrational. She had permission to be here.

She hauled in a huge breath and strode toward the aging sedan. "Hey, that's my car!"

The man straightened and looked in her direction. Their eyes met for an instant, and she shuddered at his feral, hunted expression. *That's how I look,* she thought. He slammed the door and ran before she had a chance to react further.

When he was out of sight, Laurel dashed to the car and leaned against the driver's door, looking in. The glove compartment gaped open. She trembled as she reached for the door handle.

"You all right, ma'am?"

She jumped and whirled around. A tall man in uniform stood behind her. On his gray shirt pocket hung a badge with his photograph that identified him as *Dan Ryan, Security*.

"A man was in my car."

The guard looked around the parking lot. "Where is he?"

"He ran that way." She waved toward the woods that edged the back of the lot. "He's gone now."

He nodded. "Did you lock your car, ma'am?"

"Yes, I'm sure I did."

Ryan examined the edges of the window on the driver's door. "He jimmied it. Did he take anything?"

"I'm not sure." Laurel gulped. "I don't think there was anything valuable in there."

Ryan peered into the passenger compartment. "Why don't you take a quick look and see if anything's missing."

Laurel hastily inventoried the car's contents and stood up beside him. "I think everything's here."

His gray eyes, almost the color of his shirt, were serious and thoughtful. "Did you get a good look at him?"

"He was thirty or so. Light hair, I think, but he was wearing a baseball cap. Dark jacket. Jeans." She realized suddenly how tall and good-looking the guard was. "He wasn't your height. He was standing by the car, and he didn't look that tall. Heavier, though."

"Okay, we'll watch in case he comes around here again." He looked into her eyes and smiled. So few people had smiled at her lately. It made the burglar seem less frightening somehow. "If you're sure you're all right…" He waited, as if he didn't want to end the conversation, but felt it was his duty.

She nodded. "Thank you for being here." She wanted to tell him she felt safe in his presence, that he had allayed her panic and brought her back to reality. But she found herself tongue-tied as she gazed into his empathetic eyes.

He reached for the door handle. Laurel got in, and he began to shut the door, then hesitated. "I think you dropped something."

She looked out as he stooped to retrieve the folded paper.

"Oh, thanks. That's probably my new job description."

"New job? Here?"

"Yes." She took it from him. "I'm not sure I'll take it. It's only part-time, updating the hospital Web site, but…" She felt her color rising. If she revealed too much, it might bring danger back into her life.

"It's not bad working here. Could lead to something better." He leaned on the car door, watching her. His stance was not aggressive, but said he was open for friendship. The uneasiness that was her constant companion simmered inside her. It would only complicate things if she made friends here. Friends were people she would have to confide in, and eventually leave behind. Dan Ryan seemed like a nice person. Friendly, likable, shaving-cream-commercial handsome and big enough to scare off burglars. Just the type she needed to avoid.

"I'll think about it." She reached for the armrest to swing the door shut.

"Take care," he said quickly. "I hope you take the job."

"Thanks." She allowed herself to look up at him one more time. His eyes were serious in the twilight, and his light brown hair looked soft and touchable. She smiled and closed the door with a pang of regret.

* * *

It was dark when Laurel pulled into her apartment complex. She parked and got out of the car, looking around cautiously. Her building was one of ten similar structures. The shrubbery and shadowy crannies between the units provided ample cover for lurkers.

She selected her key and headed up the walk. Just before she opened the door, she closed her eyes for an instant and breathed a prayer. Opening the door was always the hardest moment of her day—fearing the worst, only to be confronted by the quiet solitude of her lackluster apartment. Even after all this time, she half expected another shock to await her. Coming home and stumbling over a dead body in her living room had shattered her sense of security.

Lord, you've got to help me get over this. She pushed the door open and fumbled for the light switch as she entered. Everything seemed exactly as she had left it.

She took a deep breath. She had chosen this life. Of course, her choice had been limited. The judge had specified that she stay within a thousand miles, so she'd picked an area as far as possible from Oakland, Maine, while still meeting the court's requirements. Central Ohio. She'd waived extradition and consented to report on a regular basis to the authorities. She knew nothing about the area, except that it was well populated. But now she faced the challenges and frustrations of job hunting and meeting new people, and the mental fatigue of staying constantly on guard.

As she changed her clothes, her thoughts returned to the man who'd broken into her car. A random crime, or was it connected to the murder? Had he followed her from

Maine? The real killer still walked free while she remained accused. Her first trial had ended in a mistrial. Was she in danger while waiting for her new day in court?

She sat down on the edge of her bed to remove her shoes. For some reason the kind security guard unexpectedly popped into her mind. She remembered Dan Ryan's concern and deference. She wanted to see him again. Would it be foolhardy to take a job where he worked? Or would she be opening herself to more heartache?

After the night guard for the parking lot came on duty at ten, Dan Ryan took over an inside round, making his way through the hospital's administrative wing at an even pace. He whistled a strain of Mozart as he methodically checked all the locks. The shift passed without incident and at 11:30 p.m., he met the other inside guard in the lobby.

"How's it going?" Phil Knight called.

"The usual." Dan joined him in front of the closed gift shop. "How about you?"

"Oh, the E.R.'s busy, but nothing we need to worry about."

Dan liked the outdoor half of his shift the most, but he was glad his indoor assignment covered the part of the hospital that was mostly abandoned at night. Phil seemed to enjoy checking in with the nurses on each floor and chatting with the personnel on the graveyard shift. Dan didn't mind going alone into the empty administrative and diagnostic areas. He made it his business to know who ought to be there in the wee hours.

"Troy called in sick again?" Phil asked.

Dan nodded. He usually didn't work Mondays, but

occasionally he covered for the regular guard. He'd be tired the next day, but it was worth it. He'd certainly been in the right place tonight.

He left Phil and continued his beat, thinking of the woman in the parking lot. She was pretty, with luxuriant brown hair. That's what he'd seen first when he'd spotted her running across the lot. Brown eyes to go with it. She seemed tired and a little disillusioned. But she was young, and he could tell from her speech that she was educated. He couldn't quite place the accent.

It was hard to categorize her on such short acquaintance, but Dan had felt something when he looked into her face. She was genuine, unpretentious. She appeared to be struggling with her job situation, but he had the feeling she wouldn't give up until she found something that interested her. Of course, his track record with women wasn't the best. He'd learned he couldn't always trust his snap judgments.

He unlocked the door to Public Relations and flipped the light on. This was where she would work if she took the computer job. He wished he had gotten her name.

He sighed and turned away. If things went the way they usually went for him, she would find a better job somewhere else, and he would never see her again. No sense wondering if she was everything she seemed.

As Laurel settled into her new job, she found that each evening she listened for the security guard to make his rounds while she typed up articles and lists of medical support group meetings. By the third night she recognized the step of the evening guard, Troy Buckle, and didn't turn around as he came through the door to Public Relations.

"Howdy."

Reluctantly, Laurel glanced up. Troy was blond and attractive. He looked about sixteen, but she had learned that he was a student at the community college. In spite of her reserve, Troy made small talk every time he came through the office wing and already Laurel knew more about him than she wanted to know.

"Hi." She turned back to the monitor, hoping he would take the hint and keep moving.

"So who's the employee of the month?" He bent close to look over her shoulder.

Laurel stiffened. "Carol Marle in hematology."

"How come the security people are never employees of the month?"

She shook her head and kept typing.

"Guess I'd better hoof it. We're short one guy tonight." Troy straightened but didn't move away.

"Where's Dan Ryan, anyway?" Laurel nearly bit her tongue. She'd wanted to ask the question ever since she'd started the job, but had managed so far to suppress it.

"Dan Ryan?"

She winced, struggling between her desire to know more about Dan and her aversion to encouraging Troy. "The guy who did this shift Monday."

"I think he only works weekends, unless somebody's sick. I was off Monday, so he probably filled in for me."

"Oh." She felt foolish for asking. If he only worked weekends, she probably wouldn't see him.

"Will you be here every night?" Troy asked.

She pretended she didn't hear him, but he came around and leaned on her desk.

"Monday through Friday," she said without looking up. "I'm very busy, Troy."

He straightened again and stepped toward the doorway. "Well, I'll see you."

She said nothing, feeling only a twinge of guilt. When she went for coffee a few moments later, he was gone.

The following Monday, Laurel heard the guard approaching as she worked. She groaned inwardly. Troy had become a nuisance and over the weekend she had tried to come up with some way to discourage him.

"Hey! You signed on!"

She whirled around at the deeper, more vibrant voice. Dan Ryan smiled and strode toward her. Laurel was shocked by the excitement that whirled through her when their eyes met.

"Well, hello. I thought you only worked weekends."

"I think the regular guy has an aversion to Mondays," Dan said. "He misses at least two a month."

"That would be Troy."

"Yeah. They call me when he's out, but I've never met him. So, how's it going with the Web site?"

"All right." His steady gaze gave her a totally different feeling than the one Troy inspired. She looked away. "I'm usually gone by now, but I had a lot of pictures to upload tonight."

"So do you like doing this?"

She shrugged. "It's kind of boring."

He glanced at his watch. "I need to punch the clock down the hall. I…uh…what's your name?"

She hesitated, then self-consciously touched the new security badge clipped to her blouse. "Laurel Wilson."

"Laurel. I'm Dan. If you need someone to walk out to your car with you when you finish…"

He looked reserved all of a sudden, and she found his gentle approach very attractive.

"I'd like that. I don't think I'll be much longer."

"I'll come back in about fifteen minutes and see how you're doing."

"Thanks."

She watched him walk out into the hall. The uniform suited him, even if he was only a part-time rent-a-cop. His impeccable posture would fool anyone.

She turned back to the computer, mentally scolding herself for daydreaming about a man she didn't know. Dan was being kind to a stranger. But something deeper in his gray eyes set her heart racing. Laurel hadn't felt such pleasurable anticipation in years, and a wave of guilt washed over her. Was it possible for a twenty-eight-year-old woman to have a schoolgirl crush? Even if it were possible, the point was moot. She couldn't start a relationship now, with her life on hold.

Then there was the name thing. With the judge's permission, she had reverted to her maiden name. It had been impossible for her to find employment in Maine using the name Laurel Hatcher. Going back to Wilson gave her a little distance from the criminal case. That and the move to Ohio seemed to have worked, and she was now supporting herself, although in a rather spartan manner. But she still felt guilty and disloyal every time she gave her name.

Her fingers flew over the keyboard. It surprised her

how much she wanted Dan to like her. Was it just because she had been so alone?

She was shrugging into her jacket when he returned.

"All set?" he asked.

"Yes." She turned off the lights and locked the door, and they walked together toward the lobby in silence. She wondered if he felt as nervous as she did. There was no one on the front desk. The automatic door was shut off at night, and Dan opened it for her.

"Where are you parked?"

"On the upper level."

Outside, they mounted the long flight of concrete steps that led to where her Toyota waited under a streetlight.

"So, Laurel Wilson," Dan said as they climbed the stairs, "are you from around here?" She detected a hint of interest in his husky voice.

"No, I just moved here, and I'm still getting acquainted with the city."

"The streets can be confusing until you get used to them," he said.

She stopped beside the Toyota and glanced up at him, then put the key in the lock. "Thanks."

"Anytime." He lingered, and she hesitated to open the door. She had come to Ohio determined not to form attachments, looking for anonymity. But the solitude weighed her down, and she felt the need for a friend. She wanted to talk to someone again without being afraid. Was Dan that person?

"I guess I'll see you next Monday, if Troy is sick," she said.

He chuckled. "I'd rather not leave it to chance."

She caught her breath but didn't say anything.

"Can I call you?"

She looked out over the silent parking lot, trying to sort her feelings. She reminded herself that she ought not to get involved with a man. Dan was friendly without being pushy, and he seemed decent. She wasn't ready to tell him about her past, yet she wanted to know more about him. What kind of friendship could they form on that basis? Better to brush him off now than to have to explain things later.

When she opened her mouth to turn him down gently, she made the mistake of looking into his intent gray eyes once more.

"How about I take your number instead?" She rummaged in her purse for a notepad, and he produced a pen. As he jotted his phone number on the paper, she wondered if she was flirting with danger by being so receptive to this handsome stranger.

But at least the ball was in her court now and she could decide whether or not to make contact with him again.

Midday on Wednesday, Dan began filling out report forms on his clipboard while his partner, Jessica Alton, drove the squad car toward the police station. But completing reports on the calls he and Jess had responded to that afternoon didn't keep his mind off Laurel Wilson.

The last time he'd seen Laurel, he'd read attraction in her eyes, but her slight reserve intrigued him. For a moment while they stood by her car, he was sure she would politely brush him off. When at last she'd taken his phone number, he'd sensed a little apprehension. Of course, she hadn't called him yet. If she did, he would have to show her that she could trust him.

But did he really want that? Jumping into a relationship

too quickly could lead to disaster. He should practice the same caution she did. He sighed and flipped to his notes on the domestic disturbance he and Jess had helped defuse an hour ago.

Jessica glanced over at him. "You okay?"

"Yeah, just tired."

He'd been thinking about Laurel far too much since her car was broken into ten days ago. How much did he know about her? He didn't want his emotions to run away with him. Been there, done that. He didn't want to do it again. Mentally he made a list of crucial things he had to know about Laurel before he let himself care too much.

Laurel closed her trunk and carried her bag of groceries toward her ground-floor apartment. The overcast sky had an amber haze. The apartment buildings crowded so closely together she couldn't tell where the sun was hiding.

She shivered and looked around for movement that didn't belong in the peaceful scene. *I've got to quit being so jumpy.*

Her thoughts slid to Dan. She wanted to call him, but had held off. In her worst moments, she knew it was foolish to get close to anyone now. Yet she felt a flicker of hope when she thought of him. She stepped toward her apartment door and froze. It was open slightly, just off the latch.

The pulse in her throat raced, and she made herself take a deep, shaky breath. After a moment she reached out with one finger and pushed the door gently, another three inches. She listened, but heard nothing. Leaning to one side, she stared through the gap, but could see nothing beyond the bare, off-white wall of the entry.

Lord, I can't do this again.

Resolved that she must, she pushed the door wider and took one step then another into the entry. Through the doorway ahead, she glimpsed books, papers and an afghan strewn across the living room carpet. She stopped and closed her eyes for a moment. Her chest hurt. Images of the old house in Maine swam across her mind. The blood. The pistol. Bob's still form.

Panic rose in her. She ran for the door. The grocery sack fell from her hands as she exited. She leaped down the steps toward her car.

TWO

A man came out of the unit across the drive from Laurel's, and she hesitated only a second. He was neatly dressed, in khakis and a plaid sports shirt. His curly dark hair had a sprinkling of gray, and he was talking on a cell phone. He looked up in surprise as Laurel dashed toward him.

"Please call the police," she gasped.

"Hold on." He lowered the phone. "Can I help you?"

"Yes! Call the police, please. Someone's broken into my apartment."

"And you are?"

She gulped. "I'm in 357. Just call them. *Please.*"

He looked across the driveway, then back at her, appraising her as he brought the cell phone back to his ear.

Laurel winced. He was no doubt cataloging her wild eyes and hysterical demeanor.

"I'll call you back," he told his listener, then broke the connection, pressed a button and spoke into the phone again. "Yes, my name's Richard Hamilton, in Sherwood Apartments. One of my neighbors has had a break-in. Could you send someone out?"

"Thank you," Laurel said.

He nodded and stayed on the line, giving the address. She went to stand by her car, staring at her open front door. The terror had receded now that help was on the way. She was sure the burglar was gone.

He picked the wrong place to ransack, she told herself. Everything of value she owned had been stripped from her long ago.

She heard footsteps behind her and whirled, her adrenaline surging. Hamilton was crossing the driveway.

"I was just on my way out," he said. "The police will be right here. Would you like me to stay until they arrive?"

"I…I should be all right."

He nodded, and his concern calmed her a little. It was nice to know there were people in the complex who would help a neighbor in distress.

"Should I call the superintendent?"

She glanced back toward her building. "I don't know yet. I haven't been inside. The door was open, and—" She looked away. Kind neighbors would evaporate as soon as they learned her history. "Thank you. I'll be all right."

"I didn't get your name."

Laurel felt her lower lip tremble and she bit it, hating to give out her maiden name. He was staring at her. Surely he didn't recognize her face? How much publicity had her case received outside New England?

A patrol car turned in at the entrance to the apartment complex, and she felt light-headed with relief. "They're here." She managed a smile. "I appreciate your help."

He opened his mouth as though he would say more, but Laurel stepped away from him, waiting for the police car to draw up beside her sedan. Two officers got out and turned toward her.

"Laurel!"

"Dan?" She stared at him, stunned.

"We got a call for a burglary."

"That was me."

"Again?"

She winced.

"Sorry." Dan walked toward her. "Tell me what happened."

"Dan, I had no idea—" She broke off, eyeing his uniform with the city patches, badge and pistol. Alarm bells clanged inside her, even though it looked good on him. She'd been stupid to encourage his interest in her. A cop was the last thing she wanted in her personal life.

"I was going to tell you. Can we talk later?"

She nodded. "That's my apartment. I came home from the store, and the door was open."

A female officer rounded the car. "I'll go check on things inside."

"Laurel, would you like to sit in the cruiser while you wait?" Dan asked.

"Do I have to?"

"No. You could sit in your own car. It may be a few minutes."

She nodded and got into her Toyota without looking at him. Nausea engulfed her and she willed her heart to slow down.

Dan stepped carefully over the apples and canned soup that had rolled out of her bag on the steps and went inside.

After ten long minutes, the second officer came out and approached her car.

"I'm Officer Alton. We've determined that there's no one inside, ma'am. You can come in, but please don't touch anything."

Some of the neighbors watched from their windows. Laurel kept her head down as she followed the police officer inside.

A dull ache spread through her body as she stood just inside the living room surveying the mess. Shock was beyond her. Shock was what she had felt two years ago when she came blithely home from a shopping trip and found her world shattered. Now, a resigned defeat crept over her.

Dan stood close behind her. "I know this is stressful. Take your time, and just try to tell us if anything is missing."

She took a half step away from him. "I don't know where to start."

The carton of books she had yet to unpack lay in a jumble on the rug. Her art supplies were strewn among them, and the cushions had been tossed away from the sagging couch. Cyan acrylic paint oozed from its tube onto her favorite afghan and the gold carpet, where it seemed someone had stepped on it. Through the bedroom door, she could see clothing and bedding heaped on the floor.

"Did you have any valuables?" Officer Alton asked. "Jewelry, cash, credit cards, artwork?"

Laurel shook her head.

"Electronics?"

"My computer." She stepped quickly to the rickety desk

that held her computer setup. It was the first thing she had unpacked after making her bed.

"Is it damaged? Any peripherals missing?"

"No. All I had was the printer and—" She stopped, looking at the empty plastic box. The software disks were scattered on the desktop, and a few lay on the floor.

"At least they didn't break them," Alton said.

Laurel saw one disk peeking from under the pile of spilled books.

"You think kids did this?" she asked.

"We don't know yet."

Dan stepped closer to her. "How long were you away?"

"Maybe an hour. I just needed a few things at the store."

He nodded. "Did you have a television and DVD player here? We didn't find those."

"No."

"CD player? Radio?"

She shook her head. She hadn't had the money to buy more than the basic necessities. The apartment came furnished with the castoff sofa and desk, a wobbly single bed and a chipboard dresser. Decent furniture and an entertainment system were distant goals that were of little importance to Laurel.

"How about in the kitchen? Microwave?"

"I don't have one. I just moved here, and I didn't bring much."

Dan's eyes were thoughtful as he wrote in his small notebook. "So as far as you can tell, nothing was taken?"

She hesitated. "I can't really say yet, but I didn't have anything of value to anyone else."

"No weapons?"

She turned and stared at him. *He knows,* she thought. *He ran my name through a national database, and he knows I'm not allowed to own a gun.*

"Sorry. We have to ask."

"Nothing like that."

Dan nodded. "All right. I'm going to call for technicians to check for fingerprints around your bedroom window."

She exhaled carefully. "They came in from there?"

"Looks like it. Cut the screen in the bedroom and left through the front door. You said it was open. We'll question the neighbors in case somebody saw something."

He went out and Officer Alton said, "If you discover later that something is missing, let us know." She took a business card from her shirt pocket and held it out. "That's the dispatcher's nonemergency number at the police station. Just ask for me or Officer Ryan by name and they'll contact us."

"Thank you."

"Is there someplace you can go for now?"

"I thought I'd clean up."

"Let the techs finish before you move anything. They may want to dust those computer disks and some of the other things."

"How long will it take?"

"Could be an hour or two. You might want to go out and get lunch." The officer looked around, and Laurel noted the stark room and her meager belongings.

The thought of leaving her possessions exposed like this repelled her. At least one person had already handled them. Now a team of professionals would come in and sift through them. She didn't want to leave, but she didn't want to watch, either. When they were done, she wouldn't waste a moment in setting things to rights.

Dan saw Laurel leave the apartment and met her on the walkway. Her shiny hair fluttered in the breeze, and her troubled brown eyes radiated hurt. Of course, she was a crime victim, but something else seemed to be bothering her. He sensed it had something to do with him.

"I should have told you I'm a police officer," he said.

She shrugged and looked away.

"Sometimes people are intimidated when they find out I'm a cop. I wanted to get to know you without that being a factor. I would have told you soon." He tried to smile. "I ran some data just now and learned a lot about you."

Laurel caught her breath and stepped back. "Such as?"

Dan watched her in surprise. "Such as, you've never had a traffic violation in the state, but you've only held an Ohio license for three weeks."

"That's true."

"So, it leads to other questions."

She pressed her lips together, and Dan's training kicked in. He had a sudden conviction that she was afraid. Not afraid of burglars, but of him.

"Laurel, I thought the car burglary at the hospital last week was a random thing, but now your new apartment is broken into. Nothing was taken either time. That's very odd."

She wouldn't meet his gaze. "I don't have anything valuable."

"Apparently someone thinks you do."

Her mouth went hard, and she said nothing. Dan considered pressing the issue. He was walking a fine line between helping a woman he was beginning to care about and rooting out the truth. He didn't want to break her trust, to drive her away, but he couldn't let that cloud his judgment as a police officer. What did he really know about her, after all? Next to nothing, and that was her choice.

He decided to take a softer tack. "You said you'd call me. How about if we get together instead? I'm off duty at five. We could grab a bite to eat and talk."

"I don't think that would work." She wouldn't meet his eyes.

She was shutting down on him.

"Please?"

She shook her head. "I don't think so."

"I'm sorry." He knew she was right. He shouldn't socialize with the victim in a case he was investigating. Maybe he should have Jessica take over Laurel's case and remove himself from it.

"If I weren't the investigating officer, would that make a difference?" he asked softly.

She looked him in the eye. He waited, sensing her mental deliberation. Had he been too official, too abrasive or just too neutral? Had the uniform and the computer check built a fence between them?

"I...do want to see you again. I'm just...a little overwhelmed right now."

"Okay." Dan took a deep breath. All was not lost. "How about if I just call you, then? I'll use the number you listed in the police report."

She nodded. "Make it tomorrow. That will give me a chance to think about things."

Her restless eyes avoided him. There was apparently some sort of struggle still going on beneath the surface. "Okay. I need to help Jessica. If you think you'll be all right—"

"I'll take Officer Alton's advice and go out for lunch."

"Sure." He smiled at her, and her wistful return smile made his stomach lurch. "Be careful."

Trepidation filled her eyes. "You don't think someone would follow me?"

He wished he'd said nothing. "No. They haven't attacked you, just your property. But…stay alert."

"Will you be here when I come back?"

"Probably not. But I'll let you know later if we find out anything."

She nodded.

"I'll talk to you tomorrow, then." He opened the door of her car for her, and she backed out of her spot. He watched until she turned onto the main road.

Laurel was an enigma and, for some compelling reason, she stirred his protective instincts. He wanted to take her in his arms and assure her that everything would be all right. She had an air of vulnerability about her, yet she always stayed on guard. He aimed to find out why.

Laurel bought a sandwich at the drive-through window of a fast food restaurant and then sat in the parking lot with her car doors locked. Someone who wanted to hurt her might be watching her this very minute, and she wouldn't take a chance by getting out of the car. She sank lower in the seat as she opened the paper bag.

Dan was a cop. She should end it now, tell him she didn't

think they should pursue a personal relationship. And why hadn't he learned about her legal status when he did the computer check on her? Maybe the Ohio State Police hadn't entered the data in their computer network yet. She had checked in with them in Columbus when she first arrived, but apparently Dan had turned up nothing but her new driver's license. Maybe using her maiden name had thrown him off track, as she'd hoped it would nosy strangers.

She stared at her chicken sandwich. Her appetite had deserted her, and she regretted spending money for the food. Her budget was tight on her meager wages.

A headache began at the base of her skull. She forced herself to eat, wondering how soon she could go home.

Home. The apartment was one cell in a honeycomb of modern brick buildings. Angles and walls stuck out in staggered tiers. More privacy, but less security.

For three weeks she had told herself she would get used to her new quarters, but every time she unlocked the door, she felt as though she were entering a storage closet. No use remembering the comfortable, sprawling Queen Anne house, with its turret and wraparound porch that oozed charm. She would never have a home like that again.

Her lack of personal belongings robbed her apartment of warmth. Art on the walls, that's what it needed. Colorful throw pillows and shelves to display her books. She determined to clean up the mess, frame a couple of her drawings and buy a bookcase. And she would scour yard sales on Saturday and come home with some pretty knickknacks.

Family photos would help. Only a few had survived the fire that ripped through the family home while she was in college. But losing photos was far down her list of griefs. The fire had claimed her father's life.

She had a few snapshots of herself and Bob, but Bob was gone now, too. When her trial ended with no verdict and she was released from jail a year and a half after his death, their large wedding portrait was missing. She assumed his mother had appropriated it. The framed five-by-seven on her dresser was her strongest reminder of Bob now. She looked hard at it every day when she got up, determined not to forget him. Was it still there, in the chaos the burglars had left?

The sudden thought that the police officers might find something revealing made her mouth go dry. She should never have called them. She ought to have steeled herself and gone inside alone. Now it was too late. What in the apartment would identify her as an accused murderer temporarily freed by a hung jury? Would whatever they found tell Dan and his partner what happened in Oakland, Maine?

"You know this woman?" Jessica sifted through the clothing on the bedroom rug.

"I just met her last week. She's got a night job at the hospital."

"She's very attractive."

Dan smiled vaguely. "Like I said, we just met."

Jessica picked up a spiral-bound notebook and opened it. "Is she an artist?"

Dan looked over at the pencil drawing Jess was staring at. He reached for the sketchbook. A floppy-eared puppy wriggled on the page. "Looks like it."

He flipped through the book. A sailboat, a curly-haired child, flowers. Lots of flowers and ferns. The drawings were good enough for a botanical field guide.

"Her car was rifled last week in the hospital parking lot."

Jessica glanced at him. "She told you just now?"

"No, I was there. She didn't know I was a sworn officer. Thought I was just plain security."

"Ah. That explains her attitude when we arrived."

"Partly."

"She didn't report the car incident?"

"No. She scared him off. He didn't take anything."

"What do you make of it?"

"Nothing yet."

"But you don't think it's coincidental."

Dan sighed. "Maybe something was taken after all, and she didn't realize it. If the burglar found something with her address on it—say an envelope—it would be easy for him to come here and break in. And she might not miss a used envelope."

Jess nodded. "That's probably it. The two burglaries are connected."

Dan couldn't quite ignore the theory that the thief was searching for something specific. The way Laurel's things were tossed about suggested that. There was no nuisance damage, the way kids did when they trashed a place for the fun of it. No broken glass, no graffiti on the walls.

This was more like a deliberate but hurried search. The terror in Laurel's eyes when he'd suggested as much made him suspect he was right. She had just moved to Ohio. Computerized national databases were woefully incomplete. He could learn more if he tried, but it would take a lot of time and effort.

The technicians arrived, and Dan instructed them to lift fingerprints at the points of entry and exit, and on Laurel's belongings.

"We'll need her prints for comparison."

"She'll be back soon," Dan said. "Take them then." He and Jess headed outside to begin canvassing the neighbors. "I may check into this further," he told Jess.

"Of course."

"No, I mean Laurel. Her background. She's not from Ohio. She had to come from somewhere, but she didn't volunteer where."

"You thought this break-in was the result of a thief gaining information during a random car burglary."

"Maybe. Or maybe it's part of a bigger pattern."

"You think she's hiding something?"

Dan nodded grudgingly. "She doesn't want to talk about the past, that's for sure." What was it that she didn't want him to know? She'd dodged his questions several times now. *How bad can it be?* A dozen possibilities ran through his mind. Illegal alien? Illegitimate child? Fatal disease? Rebellious youth?

"Maybe she's in a witness protection program." Dan laughed. It sounded ridiculous, even to him.

Jess eyed him pensively. "Could be she just had a rotten week."

"I hope so."

They were halfway down the walk, and Dan realized he still held Laurel's sketchbook. He flipped the pages quickly, not knowing what he hoped to find there. The last drawing stopped him cold. She had sketched a view from a window, a view of a fenced yard. The fence was high, and the window was barred.

THREE

On Friday, Laurel called her parole officer in Augusta, Maine. "Mr. Webster, this is Laurel Hatcher."

"Good morning, Mrs. Hatcher. Are you still at the same location?"

"Yes. I'm settling into my job."

"Good, good. Still using your maiden name?"

"Yes, sir."

"No changes in address or telephone since last week, then?"

"No. I expect I'll be a here a while. Well, until…you know."

"Yes. Don't forget to report to the police out there again before the end of the month. Your attorney or I will notify you immediately if anything changes here."

"Thank you." She hung up and stared at the phone. Should she have told him that her apartment had been ransacked? Then again, what could he do about it? If anything, he could recommend she be forced to return to Maine. She had temporarily escaped the hatred and rejection she'd found there. If it were up to her, she would forget about Maine and put the past behind her.

Mr. Webster was a link to her old life. No matter how hard she tried to forget, on Fridays she had to remember.

A defiant impulse coursed through her. What would happen if she didn't call in one Friday? Would they track her down and pick her up again? She desperately wanted to melt into the dense population here and truly start over, shedding the past completely.

Even as the thought came, she dismissed it.

She had given her word. Behind Mr. Webster loomed a large legal bureaucracy that would relentlessly hunt her down if she failed to keep her promise.

Besides, she didn't want to live a lie. It was bad enough having to keep things from people without making up a false background. But she had to go on being who she was, even if it exposed her to scrutiny. Her faith in God would sustain her. It had to.

The phone rang as Laurel was opening the bottle of ibuprofen. After spending most of Thursday afternoon and Friday cleaning her apartment, she wasn't ready for Dan's call. She'd thought all afternoon what she would say to him, but she still had no words to explain her chaotic situation. Her head pounded, and she managed to down two tablets before she snatched up the receiver.

"Hello." The fatigue came across in her voice.

"Laurel? Are you all right?"

"Sorry, Dan. I was up late at work last night, and I didn't sleep well."

"I'm sorry. I wanted to update you on the investigation. We didn't get any fingerprints, other than yours and your building super's."

Several frightening possibilities presented themselves. Allowing the police department technician to take her fingerprints the day before had brought on intense anxiety.

"And?" Her voice squeaked.

"You're not in the system, but then you knew that."

He doesn't know yet! She exhaled carefully. "Do you think the superintendent broke in? That doesn't make sense. He has a key."

"No, we checked, and he did some maintenance and repairs on your unit this spring before you moved in. When the techs checked around the window, where the screen was cut, that's all they found."

"So…" She put her hand to her forehead, where the headache had migrated and taken up residence.

"Gloves. It's all we can figure."

"Oh. Of course."

"I'm sorry you're having such a rough time."

She was silent for a moment, soaking up the gentle concern in his voice. "Thank you. I just need some quiet time to put things in perspective."

"I was hoping we'd get some good prints so we could check the database."

"How extensive is that database?"

"It's for the entire state of Ohio."

"Impressive."

"Well, we have access to national databases, too. But without any clear prints from the suspect…"

Laurel gulped, but could not bypass the lump in her throat to answer him. If he ran her prints through the national database, he would have a shock.

"I wish you didn't have to work tonight," he said. "I'd

take you someplace quiet. How about Sunday?" His quiet voice sounded tentative but hopeful. "There's a place I'd like to take you. It's peaceful."

Laurel closed her eyes. Would it be so foolish to get close to someone like Dan? More than anything, she wanted to accept his invitation. "Where is it?"

"My church."

Something good and sweet burst over her, and she lay back against the hard arm of the sofa. "I'd like that."

Dan sighed, as though he had been holding his breath, waiting for her reaction. "You don't think that's corny? A lot of people are turned off when they find out I go to church, and when they learn that I go three times a week if I can, they think I'm some kind of cult fanatic."

"It's the sanest thing I've heard since I moved to Ohio," Laurel said.

"It's not a big church, but it's good. Do you…go to church?"

"I visited one a couple of weeks ago, but it wasn't right for me." She repressed the memory of when she slipped into the auditorium just after eleven o'clock, thinking she would find a back seat. The large church was more than half full, and no seats were open near the back. Her pulse raced, and she felt hot all over. An usher appeared to guide her down the aisle. The prospect of being stared at by so many people terrified her, and she choked out, "Excuse me," and bolted out the door.

"Haven't found the right one?" Dan asked.

"Not yet."

"Try this one. I'll pick you up Sunday morning."

Apprehension sprang through her again. If only he

weren't a police officer. Everything else about him seemed perfect. So perfect that she wanted to take the chance it would work. And attending his church would tell her a lot about him. She took a deep breath and tried to sound light-hearted. "Why not?"

"Fantastic. Nine-thirty? We'll go to Sunday school."

"I'll be ready."

"Laurel, I need to talk business for a minute."

"What is it?" She rubbed her temple with her fingertips, trying to ease the dull pain.

"I can see that you value your privacy, and I know this investigation has been difficult for you. I'm truly sorry. But if there's anything else you remember that will help us find out who did it, please tell me. That man in the hospital parking lot, too. If the two crimes are related—"

Laurel clenched the receiver. "What if we just forget it?"

There was a silence. "I…can't do that, and I'm not sure I want to. I want to know there's not more to this, and I want to be reasonably certain it won't happen again."

She heard her own choppy breath and pulled away from the receiver for a moment so he wouldn't hear it. "Please, Dan, I just want to get on with my life."

"I'm just trying to solve this burglary, so you can feel safe again and not worry when you come home from work at night."

"Sometimes it's easier to let things go." She knew that wouldn't make sense to someone as practical as Dan.

"If I knew they wouldn't bother you again, I'd consider that. Maybe you should get a roommate."

"No," she said quickly. "Too invasive."

"You've got a point. I suppose you could get a dog."

She smiled involuntarily, but she knew she wouldn't get one. Pets tied people down. If she had to move suddenly, she couldn't be encumbered by a dog. *Or a man,* she thought, but firmly squelched that notion.

"Let me give you my cell phone number."

Another thread binding them together, barely perceptible. "All right, if you want to."

"I do. If anything happens, please call me directly. Laurel, I don't want you to be afraid."

She drew in a breath. "I'm not. Honest."

"That's good. I want you to feel secure and I hope having me just a phone call away helps."

"It helps more than you realize, Dan."

When they had hung up, she set her alarm clock and lay down on her bed for half an hour. The headache receded at last, but she still couldn't sleep. What was she getting herself into? Already Dan was digging into the past, and her reluctance to have him do that made him suspicious.

But already her impressions of Dan were strong enough to be called feelings, and that troubled her. They were becoming confused with her residual feelings for Bob. Maybe it was too soon.

The broader implication of the conversation also worried her. Had someone followed her here? She wouldn't have thought it likely, but she'd had two incidents in a short time. Any cop would find that significant. Why would thieves target a penniless woman? Dan would find out. She knew he would. Maybe it would be better to just tell him, but how would he react?

She rose to get ready for work. As she rummaged in

the drawer for clean socks, the picture on the dresser drew her attention.

Bob. Losing him had been so hard. The trauma that followed his death had destroyed her confidence, her security, her trust—everything that mattered except her faith, and she had nearly lost that.

She picked up the frame and looked at herself and Bob, radiantly happy, six months into their marriage. Her throat ached and tears filled her eyes.

It's been a long time, she told herself. *Lord, it hurts so much to remember, but I don't want to forget.*

Would she ever be able to feel really comfortable with another man? Did she want to? Explaining her life to anyone would take a monumental effort and at this point she wasn't sure she had it in her to risk her heart again.

When Laurel woke on Saturday, the prospect of the weekend ahead nudged her to action.

She'd seen a notice for a rummage sale at the YMCA downtown. Who knew what she might find there? Ten dollars was the limit she'd set for mad money. She would buy the best bric-a-brac available within her budget.

And tomorrow…

She refused to imagine a negative outcome from her date with Dan. She eagerly anticipated attending church, and Dan would be a buffer between her and the congregation. Would the pastor be like her old pastor in Maine? Losing her church family was a tremendous regret. But she had followed her lawyer's advice after her release and lived in virtual seclusion, not contacting anyone in Oakland. Now she wondered if Jim Hight hadn't been a bit overzealous.

Two years!

Two years since she had been an active member of a church. And Dan was about to give that back to her. It was too wonderful. Something would happen to ruin it.

Before she left for her shopping expedition, she put on sunglasses and a cap. No sense being conspicuous, even at a rummage sale.

When she returned that afternoon, she was content. Not only had she found some African animal carvings and a lovely Bavarian vase at the rummage sale, but a small pine bookcase lay in the trunk of her car.

She took the small items in first. Standing in the doorway for a moment, she scanned the living room. She always followed this precursory assessment with a quick glance into the bedroom and kitchen. Belongings neat, windowpanes and screens intact. She sighed in relief and turned to the bathroom. A quick check there and she would bring in the bookcase.

Her gaze flicked first to the shower, where she always left the curtain pushed back so she could instantly know that no one was concealed there. She'd told herself this was silly, but it kept her heart from racing in fear, so she did it.

As she moved, her reflection in the mirror over the sink drew her eye. Black letters scrawled on the glass stared back at her. Her chest tightened, and she froze in place. The message registered in her brain and the air rushed out of her lungs.

DON'T FORGeT YOUR FRieNDS.

Dan jogged up the steps to the hall where his string ensemble rehearsed every Saturday afternoon. In exchange for free use of the hall, they performed at an annual benefit concert for the Lions Club.

He greeted the others cheerfully and set his violin case down. Joe Cooper helped him arrange the chairs and music stands.

"How are you doing, Dan?" Judy Nichols asked.

"Fantastic."

"What's her name?" Joe blurted out and they all laughed. Dan grinned, too, and Joe eyed him suspiciously. "Tell me there's really a girl."

"I'm planning to take her to church tomorrow." Immediately Dan wondered if the announcement was a mistake, but his friends moved smoothly from surprise to approval.

"Good for you," said Judy. "Bring her to the concert next week."

"How well do you know her?" Marcia Smith asked, opening her viola case.

"Not well. She hasn't been in the area long. I met her on my weekend job."

Marcia nodded. "I hope it works out for you."

"Thanks." Dan respected and liked the other three members of the quartet. Marcia and her husband of forty years owned a llama farm outside the city. Judy was a physician's assistant in a large medical office. Joe, closer to Dan's age, worked full-time as a city bus driver and gave cello lessons.

"I can't wait to meet her." Judy gave him the smile that always buoyed his spirits. She was the driving force behind the quartet and took charge of the music selection and performance schedule. As Dan's musical mentor, she pushed him to his limits where the violin was concerned.

Joe settled his cello into position. "So, are we ready to practice, or what?"

They were midway through the Beethoven when Dan's cell phone trilled. Although the other musicians groaned at the interruption, he knew it had to be important. Only his parents, the dispatcher and Laurel had the number. He got up and laid his violin on a chair before pulling the phone from his pocket.

"Hello?" He pressed his hand to his other ear to shut out the music.

"Dan! Something's happened."

"Laurel? Are you at home?"

"Yes. I need help."

"I'll be right there." Dan realized the music had petered out, and the three other musicians were staring at him.

Dan pushed the speed limit as much as he darted between the Lions Club's hall and Laurel's apartment. He considered calling for a patrol car to meet him there, but rejected the idea. Laurel had hung up as soon as he'd said he would come. He had no idea what he would find when he got there.

Her Toyota sat in her parking space, and he pulled his truck into an empty one near it. As he ran up the walk, he looked around. It was a quiet Saturday afternoon and nothing seemed out of the ordinary.

He rang the bell and almost immediately the door swung open. He caught his breath. Laurel's fearful eyes and trembling hands spurred him to step inside quickly, kick the door shut behind him and pull her into his arms. She broke into sobs as he held her.

"It's okay. I'm here." He stroked her long, sleek hair and caressed her shoulders. He could see nothing in the entry or the visible part of the living room that would bring on this level of anguish. Time enough to find out what happened later.

"Thank you," she managed between ragged breaths.

"It's all right."

As she sobbed, she clutched the front of his T-shirt. Dan tightened his embrace and rested his cheek on her head. He felt her hands relax slowly and her fingers splayed out on his chest.

"It's all right," he said again. "Laurel, I'll do anything I can. It's going to be okay."

She slid her arms around his waist then, and they stood holding each other for a long minute, while her sobs quieted and her breathing slowed. Dan waited, gently rubbing her back and praying silently for God to infuse her with courage.

"Come sit down." He tried to guide her toward the timeworn green sofa, but she stood back and shook her head.

"No. I have to show you first. Otherwise I won't want to."

"All right." He allowed her to lead him across the room. She stopped in front of the open doorway to the bathroom.

"In there." She stared at the floor.

"What is it?"

"Just look."

He braced himself. It had to be more than a cockroach. He fully expected to find a bloody corpse. What he saw was a spotless bathroom with white fixtures and blue tile. His quick survey took in the details, and he focused in on the medicine cabinet.

The black, handwritten letters on the mirror might have been a playful greeting, but Laurel's reaction told him they were much more sinister than that. He slid his arm around her and pulled her close to him as he read the message once more.

Laurel turned her head and buried her face against his shoulder.

FOUR

Dan felt a cold chill sweep through him as he examined the unsettling message. "Is there anything else?" he asked.

Laurel shook her head. "I don't think so. But I was afraid to open the bedroom closet."

He strode into her room and Laurel hung back. He heard her gasp as he yanked the door open. A few clothes and a plastic hanger lay on the closet floor, but otherwise it seemed perfectly normal.

"She was in here."

"She?"

Laurel swallowed. "My clothes. She went through my clothes."

"Okay. Is anything missing?"

She reached a trembling hand to slide the hangers along the closet rod, touching each item as she moved it aside. Her clothing took up only a small part of the space. Finally she dropped her hand to her side.

"My red silk blouse."

"It's missing?" he inquired.

"Yes."

"Are you certain? It's not in the laundry?"

She shook her head. "No. And she would like that blouse. It was two or three years old, but it was expensive."

"Who are you referring to?"

Laurel bit her lip. "You'll hate me."

"No, I won't."

"Yes, you will. You'll call some other cops, and you'll leave. You'll never want to see me again."

Dan pulled her back into his embrace, even though her words sent a warning shiver down his spine. "Shh. That's not going to happen."

She took a deep, tremulous breath. He turned toward the living room and pushed her gently along. "Come on. You can't stay here."

"What do you mean?"

"You've been burglarized twice. You need to get out of here before you get hurt." He pulled out his phone.

"What are you doing?"

"Calling for some on-duty officers. They can investigate this latest break-in, but you'll have to tell them what you know, Laurel."

She nodded. "Then what?"

"I'll take you to the police station. You can't stay here. They can put you in protective custody—"

"No!" Her eyes were wild with terror. "Don't do it! Please, Dan. I can't!"

He reached for her, but she twisted away.

"Don't put me in jail."

Dan frowned and tried to decide whether she was rational. "Laurel, I just want to keep you safe."

"Not in prison!"

"A safe house."

She stood still. "A place the police have for witnesses?"

"I was thinking of a friend's house. Unofficially, unless you think you need an officer's protection."

"You could hide me?"

"Maybe. If my friend agrees. Do you think you need to hide?"

She didn't answer, and his apprehension grew.

"The police department isn't likely to pay for concealing you and assigning around-the-clock protection for a burglary victim," he said. "But I know people who might give you a place to stay for a few days."

Her eyes darted about the room, and she drew in rapid breaths. At last she sank onto the sofa. "All right."

Dan gave her an approving look. "I'll find a place. If you want to pack a few things, go ahead."

"Do we have to call the police?"

Dan looked away from her desperate, beautiful face. "Laurel, I am the police."

"I know, but…"

He sat down beside her and laid the phone on the cushion between them, then reached over and took her hands in his. "I want to help. I can see that you don't want the police involved officially this time. Give me a reason not to call the dispatcher."

She didn't respond. Dan watched her silently for a minute. "Laurel, it's all right."

She shook her head.

"Yes, it is. You can trust me."

She sighed and looked at him, her brown eyes swimming in tears. "I hoped we could be friends, and if I didn't get too close, I'd never have to tell you."

"It's all right to tell me." He stroked her fingers. "I promise, I won't hate you. I can't hate you. We're way past that."

Her cheek twitched, and he was afraid she would break down again.

"If only you weren't a cop," she whispered.

Dan inhaled deeply. "Well, I am. That's not going to change. You need to tell me everything. Then maybe I can help you."

She nodded.

"How about you start by telling me where you're from."

Her face crinkled up for a second. "Maine."

He wanted to laugh and say, "There now, was that so hard?" But the look on her face warned him that she was still close to panic. "You left Maine to put something behind you."

"Yes," she acknowledged carefully.

Dan strove for a lighter note. "Hmm, broken heart, maybe? A lobster fisherman broke up with you, and you vowed never to live by the sea again?"

She shook her head soberly. "When you know the truth you won't want anything more to do with me."

"Why don't you let me decide?" He squeezed her hand. "We're not going anywhere until I know what's hurt you so badly."

Her brown eyes wavered, as if she were summoning her courage. "I've felt so guilty since the first night I met you. You see, I haven't exactly been up front with you. My last name isn't Wilson."

"I don't understand."

"It's my maiden name. I was married."

He tried to breathe evenly without showing his shock. "Okay. Want to tell me about it?"

She bit her lip.

"Divorce?" he probed gently.

She shook her head. "No. He's…he's dead."

"I'm sorry." It was a huge relief to him, but he realized it was probably anything but a relief to Laurel. He could deal with her being a widow. In time she would get past her grief, along with the guilt and anger that survivors sometimes felt. "How long ago?"

She swiped at a tear with the back of her hand. "Almost two years. I'm sorry, Dan, I should have told you, but this isn't something you tell someone the first time you meet."

"Of course not." He moved closer to her and slid his arm around her shoulders, driven by an overpowering desire to comfort her. "I'd like to help you any way I can. But if you need some time to…deal with things, that's okay. I won't push you into anything you're not ready for."

Her eyes widened in near panic, and her lower lip trembled. He wished he hadn't brought up the subject. What had happened to his resolve to exercise caution? *Way too soon, Ryan. Watch yourself.*

"Dan," she whispered, "it's a whole lot more than that. You really don't want to get involved with me."

Dan was skeptical. Being with her made him feel happier than he had felt in ages. Surely they could work through whatever problems she was fighting. He could be patient.

"Laurel, you don't know what I'm looking for in a woman."

"Fair enough. But I know what you're *not* looking for."

Before he could protest, she moved away from him and sat with her back to the armrest. "You said I wasn't in your crime database, and that surprised me. I guess they need to update it. But you should call the Ohio State Police in Columbus."

He sat very still. Crime database…she had a police record. Was that what she was telling him? It didn't shock him, after the clues she had dropped, but the sick feeling he'd had three years ago was back. He'd found a woman who had seemed perfect, and he'd soon regretfully learned otherwise. Ashleigh had almost cost him his badge and his reputation. When he'd realized she'd crossed the line into drugs, he'd tried to help her, but she wouldn't be helped. He ended it, but just in time. She was arrested a month later for trafficking in cocaine. Dan had avoided dating ever since. The pain wasn't worth it.

But Laurel wasn't like that. She couldn't be.

Something had happened back in Maine, and she had run away from it. Maybe the husband had done something and she had been implicated. Was she a fugitive? He looked at her closely. No, he couldn't believe that. Whatever she had done, she would face up to it.

"You…have a record." He didn't want to make assumptions until she told him more.

"Yes. A whopping big record. When I learned you were a policeman, I was afraid you'd find out what happened in Maine, and I didn't want that. But I also knew I couldn't be your friend without you knowing. And if it's too much for you, well, I'd be disappointed, but I really don't expect much right now."

"Whoa, Laurel, slow down."

She wouldn't look at him then, but sat shaking with her hands clenched tightly in her lap.

"What happened?"

Tears clung to her lashes as she raised them and looked into his eyes again. He hadn't noticed before that her nose was not quite straight. He fought back the impulse to slide over and kiss her. It wouldn't fix everything, but it might release the tension. He immediately regretted the thought. Kissing her was the last thing he ought to do. Time to regain his self-control. He counted silently to five as she seemed to weigh the pros and cons of giving him an answer.

Lord, You know I've got feelings for this woman. I seem to have run ahead of Your leading again. Please show me what to do. If there's a way I can be part of her life and still please You, let it happen.

"Who do you think was in your closet today?" he asked.

She bit her lip and looked toward the window. "Renee."

"Last name?"

"Chapin."

He gave her a reassuring look, urging her to continue.

She twisted her hands together. "When I first saw the message, I was just scared. But then I realized it had to be Renee."

"Can you tell me the rest? What happened to your husband?"

She took a deep breath. "I stood trial for his murder. Renee was my cellmate."

He couldn't believe what he was hearing but vowed to stay objective. "You were acquitted. You wouldn't be here now if you weren't."

It was a full five seconds before she tore her gaze away. "No, Dan, I wasn't acquitted."

Dan's mind reeled from Laurel's shocking confession that she was an accused felon. When she went into the bedroom to pack, he picked up his cell phone and debated who to call. His first thought had been his partner, Jessica, but that wouldn't do. Jess was engaged and was probably spending time with her fiancé this weekend. And she'd insist they go by the book. He hoped he wouldn't regret the decision, but until he read through the files, he would abide by Laurel's wishes and not make an official report.

After careful thought, he decided family was the place to turn tonight. If he made sure no one knew where he took Laurel, his oldest brother's family wouldn't be in danger for one night. He dialed Owen's number and waited, deliberating on how much to reveal.

Owen was curious and sympathetic. "Is your friend going to be all right?"

"I think so," Dan said. "But her apartment was broken into for the second time in two days."

"The poor woman."

"Yes, well, I was wondering if you and Marissa were feeling adventurous."

"That sounds intriguing."

Dan hesitated. "I need a safe place for Laurel while we sort this thing out. I hate to ask you. Worst-case scenario, whoever victimized her finds out she's with you. It could put you in danger."

Owen laughed. "My middle name is Cloak and Dagger."

"I'm serious."

"Well, best-case scenario, we'll hide her for a couple of days and she'll ask Marissa to be her maid of honor at your wedding."

"You're way too optimistic, but if you're willing, I'll bring her to your house in about an hour."

"I'll tell Marissa."

"Maybe I should wait while you ask her."

"Are you kidding? My wife loves company, and knowing you're finally bringing a woman around to meet us will thrill her no end."

"We're not dating, Owen. That is, not yet," he said gruffly. "Well, what I mean is…oh, forget it!"

Owen laughed. "This should be very interesting."

As Dan hung up, Laurel emerged from her room carrying a backpack.

"I've been thinking, Dan."

"What about?"

"In jail, Renee was always hinting that I was very wealthy and could take care of her when I got out. I tried to explain to her that I wasn't that well off to begin with and that if I was convicted, I would end up with nothing."

"But she didn't accept that?"

"Right. She intimidated me, I admit. The implication was that she would watch my back in prison if I would do something for her from the outside."

Dan nodded. "But you didn't."

"No. When I was released, Renee was still in jail."

"And now?"

"I don't know. I didn't want to keep track of her. But the trial was huge news in Maine. We had television privileges in jail and newspapers in the library."

"She knew that you weren't convicted."

"Yes, I expect she knew all about the mistrial. And if she were released and somehow found out I moved here…"

"Aren't the court documents sealed?"

Laurel frowned. "I thought they were kept private. But she's clever. She might have found a way to ferret that out."

"There's quite a paper trail, from what you're telling me."

"Yes. The court order in Maine, to start with, and I had to file a waiver of extradition so that I can't challenge the state of Maine when the district attorney calls for a new trial."

He cleared his throat. "Then there's the bail provision here in Ohio."

"Correct. I was afraid the state of Ohio wouldn't accept me, but Judge Elliott, back in Maine, seemed sympathetic—at least my lawyer said he was. And he didn't send me back to jail after the mistrial. I know it's unusual for a justice to allow an accused felon to leave the state on bail."

"But this judge allowed it."

"Yes, because of all the publicity and the difficulty I had finding a job after the trial."

"So you came here and somehow Renee found you."

"Evidently. No one else would have left me that message. So, I was thinking…" Her brown eyes were huge. "Dan, if Renee broke in here yesterday and threw all my clothes out of the closet, why didn't she take the blouse then?"

He was quiet in the pickup, and Laurel couldn't help wondering what was going through his mind.

"Where are we going?" she asked after ten minutes. They were headed out of the city.

"My brother's house."

She mulled that over. She hadn't thought about Dan having a family. "How many siblings do you have?"

"Three brothers, and a brat of a little sister."

"Sounds wonderful."

"Just an ordinary family."

"Exactly," she said wistfully.

Reluctantly, he changed the subject. "I need more information." He watched the rearview mirror as he turned onto a different road.

"Like what?"

"Do you have any enemies?"

She laughed without humor.

"Besides Renee, I mean." He shot her a sympathetic glance.

"Well, for starters, my in-laws, Wayne and Renata Hatcher."

"They want to see you in prison," he surmised.

"Naturally. They believe I killed their son."

"Who else?"

"It could be just about anybody," Laurel said with a shrug. "The publicity during the trial was brutal. It seemed like everyone believed I was guilty. I was screamed at, cursed and spit on. Once when my lawyer and I came out of the courthouse, people threw things at us."

Dan stared straight ahead at the highway for a long time. "How long ago was the trial?"

"It ended about five months ago."

"And you've been here a month?"

"More or less," she confirmed.

"What did you do in between?"

"At first I just hid. I didn't have any family to go to. But I needed an income, so I started looking for a job. My lawyer tried to help me, but everywhere I went I hit a brick wall. I was overqualified for janitoring, had no skills for office work and so on."

"You're here on your own recognizance?"

"Yes, that and my lawyer's ironclad guarantee that whenever the court says *jump* I will head back to Maine without delay."

"Who knows you're here?"

"No one except the probation officer, my lawyer and a police sergeant in Columbus."

Dan shook his head. "You had to check in with the police in Columbus, so it's a matter of public record. Anyone in the state police department could access the record. And doesn't your lawyer have a secretary?"

"Yes."

"Like we said before, there's a paper trail. And your probation officer must work in an office with other people."

"I…suppose so."

"Laurel, you think only three people know where you are, but the truth is there are probably dozens of people in Maine and Ohio who have access to that information. Add to that the bumble factor and—"

"Bumble factor?"

"You know—how the well-meaning but inept person inadvertently lets private information slip."

"Ah." She shrugged. "I suppose Jim's secretary might tell her girlfriend over coffee."

"Right. And the probation officer, or one of his low-paid assistants, might pocket a bribe in exchange for a tiny, seemingly innocuous bit of data."

"Not Mr. Webster."

"How do you know?"

Laurel sighed. She didn't know. It was certainly possible that her whereabouts had leaked out.

Dan put on the turn signal and drove up a long gravel driveway toward a gabled farmhouse.

"How much did you tell them?" she asked.

"Just the bare bones. I mentioned the burglaries and told Owen you need a safe place temporarily. I didn't say anything about what brought you here."

"Thank you. I don't deserve your help. I hope you don't get in trouble for not reporting the latest incident."

He braked to a stop before the two-bay garage and turned toward her. "I hope so, too."

The garage door in front of them slid up, and he eased the pickup inside. A man who looked very much like Dan stood on the step between the garage and the house. He grinned at them and put his hand up to the switch.

"Wait until the door is down," Dan said.

Laurel caught her breath. "You think we've been followed?"

"No, but we have to be careful."

He took Laurel inside and introduced her to Owen and Marissa.

"We're thrilled to have you here," Marissa said. Her shoulder-length blond hair was caught back with a barrette, and she wore jeans, a maternity top and sandals. She seemed sincere and solicitous, and Laurel liked her at once.

"Thank you. I hate to put you out, but Dan insisted I couldn't stay at the apartment any longer."

"I should think not," Owen said. He took Laurel's backpack from Dan and disappeared down a hallway.

Marissa smiled at them. "I just put Patrick to bed. Did you eat supper?"

"I can't stay long," Dan replied. "I need to go in to the police station tonight and look over some records."

"Come on. Leftover stroganoff and salad." Marissa brooked no arguments as she headed for the kitchen.

Dan sighed with resignation. "I hope you like stroganoff."

"Are you sure it's okay for me to be here?" Laurel whispered. "She's pregnant. What if—"

"It's fine." He reached for her hand, and they went together to the kitchen. Marissa was already pulling plastic containers from the refrigerator.

Owen came in behind them. "Patrick's still awake. He wants to see Uncle Danny."

Dan grinned. "Do you mind?"

"Go," said Marissa. "He must have heard your voice." As soon as Dan was out of the room, she fixed Laurel with a curious stare. "We know next to nothing. If you don't mind my asking, what happened?"

Laurel felt a blush spreading over her cheeks. "I'm sorry. If it's any inconvenience—"

"Not a bit," said Marissa. "We're happy to help. But this is bizarre behavior on Dan's part."

"How long have you been seeing Dan?" Owen asked.

"I'm not. We're just friends. That is…well, we were going to go to church tomorrow, but I'm not sure Dan will let me now."

"He told me on the phone that you need to keep your head down," Owen noted.

"Yes, and it's a little scary. Someone trashed my apartment yesterday, and today I had another intruder and some things were stolen."

Marissa's face was full of concern. "Anything valuable?"

"Not really, just a blouse and…some ice cream."

"Ice cream?" Owen laughed. "Your burglar must have a sweet tooth."

"I guess so. We almost didn't notice, but at the last minute I checked the refrigerator."

"That is so weird." Marissa put a plate in the microwave.

"What's weird?" Dan asked from the doorway.

"Laurel's burglar helping himself to a snack."

Dan shrugged. "You just never know, do you?"

"It's frightening, knowing someone came into your home like that," Marissa said.

Laurel bit her lip.

"They tried to take prints after the first break-in," Dan said, "but they didn't get anywhere. I didn't ask them to come again tonight. I decided we'd better get Laurel out, and now I'm wondering if I shouldn't have brought most of her things."

"I can help you tomorrow," Owen offered.

"Sit down. The food's almost ready." Marissa brought the plates over and set them on the table. Dan offered the blessing, and they began to eat.

"This is wonderful," Laurel told Marissa. She hadn't done any real cooking in weeks and the stroganoff tasted like a bit of home.

Owen straddled a chair and said to Dan, "So, Laurel says she might have to miss church in the morning. What do you think?"

Dan shrugged. "It's important to keep her out of sight for a while."

"She could go to our church with us," Marissa said. "She could wear some of my clothes and a big hat."

"Oh, that would make her inconspicuous," Owen said with a chuckle.

Dan leaned back. "What do you say, Laurel?"

"I don't know. I'd like to go, but if you think it's dangerous…"

"Here's what I think." Dan took a sip from his water glass and set it down. "I'm going to go read the files we talked about. Unless I find something alarming, I'll be back in the morning to pick you up. I think you'll be safe at my church, and I'm pretty sure no one followed us here tonight."

Laurel smiled. "Then let's go for it."

Dan stood up. "Sounds good. Now, if you all will excuse me, I need to hit the road."

He reached for Laurel's hand and drew her with him toward the door to the garage. "If things settle down, we'll get you back home Monday before you have to go to work," he said softly. "If not, I'll bring your computer and your other things to you."

She nodded. "I'd hate to lose my computer." Another dart of anxiety hit her. "Do you think my car is all right in the parking space?"

"I'll ask the patrol sergeant to send a unit through Sherwood Apartments several times tonight. That may help."

She looked up into his eyes, and the enormity of it hit her. "Dan, why would anyone do this to me? Renee I can almost understand. She thought we had an agreement, although it was all one-sided. Now she's angry that I didn't follow through. But the rest of it—I don't get it."

"Me, either. Someone was looking for something before Renee found your place. Any way I rationalize it, that's what I come up with. An unknown burglar broke in the first time and trashed your place, then Renee came and stole your blouse and left you the message."

Laurel shook her head. "Even if someone hates me, what good can come of going through my things? I don't have anything."

"They dumped out your books and software," he reminded her.

"And my clothes and dishes. I guess I'm lucky they didn't pour flour and cocoa all over the kitchen."

Dan's brow furrowed. "Think hard about this, Laurel. Who would come all this way after you…and why?"

"I don't know! But I'm scared. And I don't want to bring trouble on your brother and his family."

"I know."

"If I can't go home soon, I certainly can't stay here and put them in danger. Imagine someone breaking into their home."

Dan sighed. "You're right. We'll figure something else out. In the meantime, pray hard."

"I will." Laurel looked into his tender gray eyes. "Dan, you don't have to do this."

"I'm in it now. Just be careful. We'll talk tomorrow, after I read the files and have a better picture of your situation."

She nodded. When he could see the full picture, he would regret becoming involved, but for the time being, here she was in his brother's home. She prayed that these innocent bystanders wouldn't get caught in the cross fire.

FIVE

Dan walked into the police station with his jacket slung over his shoulder.

"Ryan! You on duty tonight?" The night patrol sergeant eyed his jeans and T-shirt in surprise.

"No, I just came in to check on something. Thought I'd use the computer for a few minutes."

The sergeant nodded and Dan went to the duty room. A couple of other officers were huddled over their paperwork. Dan sat down and turned on a computer, sending up a heartfelt prayer.

She wants me to do this, Lord. She wants me to look up the case and decide for myself what to do. All right, I will. Just give me wisdom, please.

The local law enforcement database still had no information about Laurel. He logged on to the network that gave him access to records from other states. It took a while, but finally he found what he needed.

He went after Renee Chapin's file first. She had a string of convictions for theft, burglary, criminal trespass and assault. She'd spent several short stints in the Kennebec County jail, and a longer one that he figured overlapped

Laurel's incarceration. While there, she'd racked up another assault charge and a count of trafficking in contraband. Renee had been released in February. She'd had more than two months to find the woman she thought had reneged on her promise. Dan printed out her mug shot and studied it carefully.

No use putting it off any longer. He entered the name Laurel Wilson Hatcher. The mug shots that came up on the screen hit him with terrible force. She looked so haggard, so scared. He wanted to turn it off.

Laurel Wilson Hatcher, 26, arrested on first degree murder. Husband, Robert E. Hatcher, 27, found fatally shot on the stairs in their home in Oakland, Maine. One bullet to the chest, from a nine-millimeter pistol. His own pistol. It was discovered lying at the foot of the stairs, a few smeared fingerprints on it. Some were the victim's; at least one was Laurel's.

Dan's heart went out to Laurel. She had walked in on that scene, found her husband lying dead in their home.

He read every word of the police reports. No evidence of a break-in. Laurel was clearly the main suspect from the beginning, which made sense—spouses were always the first suspects. She claimed she'd been out shopping all morning, came home and discovered the body, but no one could corroborate her story.

Motive? Her husband worked for his father in the family's construction firm. As a project supervisor, he earned a salary a cop would envy. Their house, a wedding gift from his parents, was a century-old Queen Anne. Bob drove a Corvette and was heavily insured. In all, Dan figured the widow ought to have come out a millionaire.

Of course, the insurance company wouldn't pay a death benefit to a person accused of murdering the insured.

He tried to bring up the court records, but he couldn't retrieve them. Maybe Lieutenant Powers could help him on Monday. *If* Dan decided to let him know he was looking at this. Powers was sure to be curious.

He searched for a local newspaper site and accessed its archives. The profuse details astounded him—everything from Bob's golf handicap to the brand of shoes Laurel purchased the morning of the murder. He waded through the hoopla and repetitive backstories in each article for the vital information he needed.

The initial murder investigation had lasted a few weeks, leading to Laurel's arrest and detention at the county jail. His heart ached just thinking about it. The trial preparations dragged on for nearly a year and a half. At last the trial began in superior court in Augusta, the state capital.

The prosecution had tried hard to prove its case. Robert Hatcher's mother testified against her daughter-in-law, claiming the young couple fought shortly before the murder. A friend of the victim's testified that Laurel excelled at marksmanship. He and Bob hunted together every year, and Laurel had gone along the last two years. They'd held shooting contests for fun, and Laurel knew what to do with a handgun. The friend even saw her shoot the murder weapon for sport, with deadly accuracy.

Her spotty alibi damaged the defense's case. Laurel had done her shopping in Bangor, an hour from her home in Oakland, and stopped on the way home at a picnic area. She claimed she spent at least a half hour strolling through the woods, looking for early wildflowers. Dan thought immediately of the many plants depicted in her sketchbook.

But no one could place her car at the picnic area. No one had seen her drive into the garage when she arrived home. She had dated receipts from three Bangor stores, but all the times imprinted on them were early in the day. That missing half hour at the picnic area cast enough doubt. That and the fingerprint on the gun...

It ended in a hung jury. Circumstantial evidence, and not much of it, left all kinds of room for doubt. But two of the jurors had held out for a conviction. The deliberations went on for three days, until the judge finally dismissed the jury. He declared a mistrial, but no new trial was set. Instead of sending her back to jail, the court had released her on bond. The judge allowed her to move out of state, provided she waived extradition and kept them informed of her whereabouts. She was free, for now. But when they set the date for a new trial, she would be right back in the courtroom.

Dan sat for a long time staring at the screen. The screen saver began flashing, and he turned it off.

As soon as the blank monitor faced him, he wished he'd printed it all out so he could go over it at home. He wanted to comb through it relentlessly until he found something that would exonerate Laurel.

But if such evidence existed, he wouldn't find it there.

It was nearly time for him to report to his security job. He went home and put on the gray uniform. As he drove toward the hospital, his thoughts returned to Laurel. The police thought they had the murderer, and no one was looking for the real killer. She needed a defender, someone who would stand up for her and keep her safe. Dan didn't know if he could do that, but he wanted to try. However, despite the desire to be there for Laurel, an inner voice warned, *She's a murder suspect. You know nothing about her. Criminals lie. They put on a charming front. They use people they think can help them.*

Thoughts of Ashleigh flitted through his mind—the way she'd charmed him. She'd managed to hide her darker side from him for weeks, until his heart was engaged. And when he learned her needs, he couldn't meet them. She was too deep into drug abuse for him to help her, even if she'd wanted his help.

He parked in the hospital employees' lot and bowed his head for a moment. *Dear God, I don't want to go through that kind of pain again. Help me to keep things in perspective. I don't want to be stupid and fall for a woman who has no respect for You. But Laurel…she seems to believe in You. Make me wise. Give her a resolution to this murder case, Lord. I don't want to meddle where I shouldn't, but she needs help. Please, if You can use me in her life, I'm here. Just help me not to get emotionally involved if this isn't right.*

Dan dressed carefully on Sunday in a dark-gray suit and took a long time choosing the necktie. He tied it three times before it hung to his satisfaction. He hadn't been this nervous since his six-month evaluation at the police station.

He drove slowly around the city park in the center of town, watching his rearview mirror. When he was sure he wasn't being followed, he headed for the highway and out of the city. After snatching only four hours of sleep, he was still tired but couldn't stop thinking about Laurel's predicament.

He approached Owen's house with anticipation. It would be his and Laurel's first intentional meeting, and he was eager to see how she would greet him.

She smiled when he entered, but he thought the smile was a little strained. Her dark brown skirt swirled around her calves, and she wore brown loafers. A green satin headband that matched her blouse held her chestnut hair back from her forehead. *Good,* he thought. *Not too fancy. Just a regular girl.*

When Patrick ran to him, Dan picked him up and gave him a bear hug. "Hello, buddy."

"We're just about to leave," Marissa said. "Do you need anything before we go?"

"No. In fact, we'll head out when you do."

"Will you come back for dinner?" she asked.

"I need a chance to talk to Laurel."

"You can do that here," Owen said.

Dan hesitated. "It's probably better if we don't come back here today."

Laurel's eyes widened. "I'll get my bag." She turned toward the hall.

"Is anything wrong?" Owen asked.

"No more than it was last night. It's just that I didn't realize last night quite how serious it is."

Marissa laid a hand on his sleeve. "I'm sorry."

"Anything we can do?" Owen asked.

"I don't think so, but thanks. I need to get Laurel away to a safe place."

"Dan, tell us what's going on." Owen's eyes met his with the stubborn persistence they'd both inherited from their father.

"I will when I can. Right now I need to help Laurel, and the best way I can do that is to find her another place to wait."

"What is she waiting for?" Marissa's voice cracked, and Dan suspected her nerves were fraying. He regretted that. Best get Laurel out of their house quickly.

"I promise I'll update you soon. Keep praying for us. But for now, the less you know, the better."

"You're serious," Owen said. "You're some kind of target."

"Not me. Laurel."

She came from the bedroom, carrying her backpack, and turned to her hostess. "Goodbye. Thank you for everything."

"I hope you can come back soon," Marissa said.

Owen cleared his throat. "Yes, do."

Laurel smiled, but Dan caught the glint of tears in her eyes. They went out, and Dan opened the door of his pickup for her.

"How'd it go?" he asked as he eased the truck down the driveway.

"All right. Marissa and I got along great."

He glanced at her before pulling out into the street. "She's good for Owen. I thought you two would have a lot in common."

"Thank you for arranging this, and for letting me share your family for a night."

Dan smiled. "You're welcome."

She looked over at him. "How much did you find out last night?"

"Quite a lot."

"So did I."

"Oh?"

"Yeah. Classical music. String quartet. Why didn't you tell me?"

"There's a lot you don't know about me, Laurel, and a lot I don't know about you. I want to spend more time with you and learn everything about you."

She said nothing, but she no longer flinched when he mentioned the prospect of unraveling her past. "So what else did you learn about me?" he asked, deliberately switching subjects.

Her shy glance warmed his heart. "Well, let's see. Should we begin with your love life?"

"They're anxious for me to join their state of wedded bliss," Dan said with a sigh. "No pressure."

"Right." They glanced at each other and laughed.

"Family can be very pushy," Dan said.

"Mmm. Owen said you didn't date much in school, but you've had a couple of semiserious relationships since you joined the P.D."

"Emphasis on *semi,* please."

"All right. Is Jessica one?"

"No. Jess is getting married in August. And I would never date a work partner. It's against regs, anyway. She's a good cop, though."

Laurel nodded. "Let's get down to business. You don't think it's safe for me to be at Owen's house any longer."

No dodging the topic now, he thought. "I know you don't want to put them at risk."

She nodded, her lips pressed together. "I would never forgive myself if something happened to them."

"Laurel, someone out there wants something you have."

She pounded her knee in frustration. "But I don't have anything."

"Obviously there are people out there who think differently. The way I see it, these criminals felt it was important enough to kill your husband over. There's either something that will implicate them, or something that will exonerate you. They don't want either of those things to happen."

"But why now? If there were evidence like that, you'd think they'd have tried to find it before."

"No one searched your belongings in Maine?"

"Well…" She was quiet for a long moment. "While I was in jail, Bob's and my house was stripped."

"By thieves?"

"You could say that. His parents emptied the house and sold it."

"How could they do that?" Dan asked.

"They paid for the house. They said it was theirs."

"But your furniture?"

"Sold. No explanation except that some of the things had belonged to Bob's grandparents."

"That's terrible. How did you come up with bail?"

"My lawyer arranged it after the trial. He's filed a civil suit to try to recoup the value of my belongings from the Hatchers, but it's still hanging—probably until after the criminal trial."

Dan crinkled his forehead. "What about the rest of your personal things?"

"They had my clothing and a few other things boxed up and put in storage while I was in jail. I got those, but that's it. I think they even took a few of my paintings, but why they would do that if they hate me so much is beyond me."

"You mean, paintings you did yourself?" He remembered the art supplies he'd seen in her apartment after the first break-in.

"Yes."

"Were they worth anything?" he inquired.

She looked away with a tiny shrug. "I sold a few pieces for between three and five hundred dollars each, and I won a prize at the Waterville Arts Fest the summer before. But I wasn't well-known, and now I'm less than nothing in the art world."

"Maybe not. Think about it. A painting by a convicted murderer might be worth something, especially if it's good."

She shuddered. "That's despicable."

"I'd like to see your art."

She said nothing.

"What about your husband's things? Clothes, books, sporting equipment?"

"Gone."

He pressed on. "Photos?"

"I have a few. Those and my paints."

Dan ruminated on that as he turned into the church parking lot. "Your computer."

"It's new. I took a risk and bought it when I got here. But I almost ran out of money before I got my job because of it. So there wouldn't be anything on the hard drive the killers would find useful." The intruder probably knew that, Dan reasoned. Otherwise the computer would have been stolen.

"The second trial is imminent, and there's something the killers are afraid will come out this time. So they traced you, hoping to find whatever it is that could incriminate them," Dan suggested.

"I can't believe I ever had anything like that without knowing it."

Dan parked the truck and sat still for a moment. "What other explanation is there?"

Laurel's brow furrowed. "Renee. What about her? She was definitely in my apartment. The message, the blouse…"

"True."

"And Renee had nothing to do with Bob's death. She was in jail on another charge when it happened."

"Renee is incidental. But however she found you, Bob's killers took the same route. They both learned you were here, and they came after you for different reasons."

"You must be right. I've got two sets of enemies after me."

"I'm afraid so."

The anxious frown between her eyebrows deepened. "Dan, I'm frightened."

He touched her cheek. She was telling him the truth. He could feel it. "I'm in this with you now, Laurel."

She bit her lip and nodded. "Thank you. I'd try to talk you out of it, but I don't think I'd succeed."

"You're right. I don't know what would sway a jury, but if it's out there I'll find it."

SIX

Dan tried to ignore the stares as they entered the church, but he couldn't repress a smile. The teacher was about to start the adult class in the auditorium, so no one made a scene, but he could tell everyone was curious about the lovely woman sitting beside him.

Laurel listened avidly to the Sunday school lesson, and she turned easily to the place in her Bible. Dan allowed himself to let go of his anxiety and relax against the padded pew.

Between the services, Terry Wyman stopped in the aisle with his wife, Donna.

"Hey, Dan." They shook hands, and Laurel smiled warmly as he introduced the Wymans.

Donna immediately launched into a conversation with Laurel. Dan worried that Laurel would feel smothered by Donna's enthusiasm, but she held up her end, answering the usual questions about where she lived and worked. He chatted with Terry, but tried to stay aware of how things went between the women and caught a knowing smile from Donna. She and Terry had tried several times to fix him up with nice girls they knew.

Terry leaned toward him. "About time."

"Hey, don't get overly jubilant here," Dan shot back.

"Right. But the fact that you're bringing her here is an improvement. We'd about given up hope for you."

Dan grimaced, taking Terry's comment as a veiled reference to Ashleigh. Definitely a mistake.

"I'd better go collect our daughter from her Sunday school class," Donna said a few moments later. She headed toward the back of the auditorium, and Terry settled in a pew across the aisle.

Laurel turned her face up toward Dan. "Nice people. Old friends?"

"Yeah. Terry and I were in school together, and we see each other here pretty often. He's in construction. We play some basketball together."

Her nearness ambushed him. Her imperfect nose, her creamy skin, her sparkling eyes—

She closed them precipitately, taking a quick breath. Had she felt it, too? Dan hoped she had felt *something*.

She was quiet through the worship service. He suspected she avoided looking directly at him. She murmured her thanks when he held out the hymnbook, and held her edge of it almost gingerly as they sang. Her voice was quiet, but true and clear. Did she like music? She must. Still, he felt he knew nothing about her, except that she was accused of killing her husband and must face a second trial for it.

Those were not the things Dan wanted to know about her. Despite his feeling that caution was needed, the idea of discovering all the commonplace things about her excited him. But in order to do that, he needed to see her go free.

Dan forced his mind back to the service. He knew that

at a time like this, prayer was just what he needed to bolster his spirits and infuse him with renewed purpose.

"I like your church," Laurel told Dan in the truck afterward. The pastor's message had touched her heart, and she'd felt almost at home.

"I'm glad." His eyes gleamed as he backed out of the parking spot. "Come back."

"We'll see." She hoped she could do that, but with the future so tenuous, she didn't dare consider it yet.

"I'd like to take you out to eat," he said, "but we need to keep you out of sight."

"So where are we going?"

"I called a friend last night. She's open to having you stay with her for a while."

Laurel stared at him in surprise. "I thought I was too much of a liability."

"Judy's very laid-back, and she's single. She's willing to take the risk."

Dan must know this woman well to make that decision, Laurel realized. She wondered what their relationship was. "Did you tell her everything?"

"No, just about the burglaries. But she's smart. You may want to tell her the rest before she figures it out. I'll leave that up to you."

Laurel took a deep breath. She didn't like bouncing around from place to place, depending on the kindness of strangers. "What about my stuff?"

"If you and Judy hit it off, I'll go pack it up this afternoon. You can call the superintendent and tell him you're moving out."

"If I don't clean the apartment, I'll lose the deposit."

Dan shot her a sober glance. "How critical is that?"

"I'm basically broke. My paycheck is pretty small."

He nodded. "I'll take care of it."

"You can't."

"Yes, I can. I have lots of friends who will help."

"Just take me over there for a couple of hours. I can do it."

"No," he said firmly.

Laurel watched him drive for a moment. "And my car?"

"I'll get someone to help me move it to Judy's if you want, but it might be better for you to sell it and get something else."

Laurel smoothed a wrinkle from her skirt and tried calm her racing thoughts. "You think I should change cars?"

"I'm sorry, but they know your car. If it's a killer who is after you, he won't stop at going through your things. Next time he'll want your purse or the contents of your pockets."

She swallowed hard against the lump in her throat. "You shouldn't be doing this alone."

"Do you want me to make an official report?"

She looked out the window, considering. "Would they put me back in jail?"

"I doubt it. I don't know."

"I haven't done anything."

"That might be the only way they could protect you. Or, if the commissioner thought you were too much of a headache, I suppose he might send you back to Maine."

"I'm allowed to be here," she protested.

"Not if he convinces the Maine courts that you're a liability to the people of Ohio."

He put the turn signal on, and Laurel realized they had

reached their destination. A new apprehension hit her. "What if your friend hates me?"

Dan parked the truck and turned toward her. "No chance," he whispered. "Relax."

A middle-aged woman emerged from the breezeway of the shingled Cape Cod, and Laurel took a deep breath. Judy was not at all what she had expected. But then, what did she expect? One of Dan's old girlfriends?

He lowered his window as Judy approached.

"Hi, Dan. Why don't you pull over behind the willow tree, and I'll take Laurel inside."

"Good idea."

Laurel climbed from the cab and followed her hostess into the house.

Judy closed the door behind them. "Welcome! I'm excited to have you here."

"Thank you. Dan was very hush-hush about the arrangements. I hate to put you out."

"No problem. I need a little pizzazz in my life." Judy's lively brown eyes belied the sprinkling of gray in her short hair. "Dan says you're having a rough time, and I offered my hospitality, such as it is. I'm gone a lot, and it's quiet here. He thought you'd like that."

"That's very kind of you." Laurel wondered how this woman could trust someone she'd never met with her lovely home and treasured belongings. Judy didn't seem to be the naive type, but she was throwing her private life open to a stranger in trouble. Of course, Laurel was here on Dan's recommendation. That must be it. Everyone trusted Dan. He would never bring an unsavory character into their lives. As she followed Judy to the room where she would stay, she vowed not to let Dan down.

The rich colors and functional antiques in the house charmed her. Judy's casual conversation put Laurel and Dan at ease as they shared lunch. When she learned her hostess was a physician's assistant, Laurel again felt her own inadequacy. She'd never held a job that paid more than minimum wage.

Judy smiled at her. "What do you do for work, Laurel? Seems to me Dan mentioned you work at the hospital."

"Yes. I update their Web site five nights a week."

"From home?"

"No, I go in and work there."

Judy frowned. "Surely you could do it from home. That is, if you have a computer."

"I do. And you're right—I could easily work from home."

"I know some people in administration. If you want, I can ask them about it. Under the circumstances it would be safer."

"Do you think they'd go along with that?" Dan helped himself to more salad. "Because I can bring Laurel's computer here and set it up."

"I don't see why not," said Judy. "The hospital has home health care workers with home offices. They go in once or twice a week for files on their casework."

"I'd appreciate that," Laurel said.

"Just don't let on that she's staying with you," Dan cautioned.

Judy nodded. "Don't worry. I'll be very discreet."

Laurel looked at Dan and Judy. "You're both doing so much for me, and, Dan, you have an entire life outside of this. I feel as though I'm ruining it by monopolizing so much of your time."

He shook his head. "That's not the phrase I'd use to describe what you've done to my life in the last two weeks, Laurel."

Judy arched her eyebrows and smiled. "I believe it's time for me to start the dishwasher."

"Let me help you." Laurel started to rise.

"No, you have more important things to do. You and Dan must have things to talk about before he goes on duty tonight."

"That's right. You have to work at the hospital." Again Laurel was struck by what a huge inconvenience she brought to Dan. There wasn't room in his life for her.

He reached over and squeezed her hand. "Judy's right. We need to talk, and then I'll go for the rest of your things."

Judy gathered their coffee cups and headed for the kitchen. "Make yourselves at home."

Dan stood and led Laurel into the living room. They sat down on the brown plush sofa.

"I read what I could find by computer last night," he said. "It told me enough, I think."

"Enough for what?"

"Enough to tell me you got a lousy deal."

She gave a short laugh.

"I mean it. You shouldn't have to live with it hanging over you. It's bad enough to lose someone you love—"

"How do you know I loved him?" Her voice came out tight.

Dan took a deep breath. "You must have. You would never marry a man you didn't love. Not you, Laurel."

He reached for her hand and Laurel sat still, unable to quell the thrill that his touch evoked.

"It's hard to even think about it," he said. "You went through so much. I hope you weren't alone in all of that."

Laurel's heart raced. Her feelings for Dan were growing. He was conscientious and reliable, but more than that, he was tender and compassionate. She knew that if things progressed in this direction, she would soon be helplessly in love with him.

"My lawyer tried hard," she whispered.

"How about your family?"

She shook her head. "My close family's gone. And Bob's family was…hostile."

"I gathered that much from the clippings. But you must have had a church family."

She shook her head. "My pastor was away when it happened, and I didn't dare to contact anyone. The pastor did come to see me a couple of times later on, but I told him not to come to the jail too often. After the trial, my lawyer found me a place in Portland. He told me not to contact anyone, just to let him handle lining up witnesses for the next phase."

"But how could your friends leave you alone like that?"

"People were confused, and it bothered them to have me around. I never knew who would be nice to me, and who would be mean or ignore me. I didn't want to put the pastor in an awkward position. And my lawyer thought it was best that way. After I moved to Portland I went to church a few times, but it was always to a different church."

"Is your lawyer a believer?"

She shook her head.

"How could you stand it, being alone like that?"

"I've tried not to think about it lately," she confessed. "It was pretty awful. After the trial, I wanted to go home and lock myself in, but I didn't have a home anymore. As I mentioned earlier, Bob's parents sold the house they'd bought for us. And things were so tense in Oakland, I was afraid to stay in town."

Dan stared at her. "I don't see how anyone who knew you could think you were guilty."

"It seemed like everyone thought I did it, even though I wasn't convicted, and it was just a matter of time before the court did a recount and said so. Even down in Portland, everyone knew who I was. I'd walk into a store and people would stare. I had no income. The insurance company won't settle until the case is closed, and the civil suit can't go forward. I applied for jobs, but they all wanted to know if I had a criminal record. It was just too hard."

"So the judge let you move away."

"Yes. I petitioned him, and my lawyer made a good plea for me. Convinced him it would save the state of Maine a bundle, that I'd be better off where I could live in anonymity and that I wasn't a flight risk. After a few weeks, the judge agreed to let me leave the area. I had to practically sign my life away, and I have to check in by phone every week. It's not as bad as prison, but…" She sobbed involuntarily. "If they call me back…"

He inched over next to her. "Come here."

She went slowly, but willingly, into his arms and laid her head on his shoulder. Dan let out a deep sigh.

"You should have gone back to court within sixty days," he murmured.

"My lawyer waived the time limits. He thinks that unless he comes up with some new evidence to help me, going back to trial soon would work against me."

"And nothing new has turned up?"

"So far as I know. This waiting is horrible. I'm starting to wish I could just get it over with."

"I'm so sorry, Laurel. If I could have been there—"

"You didn't know I existed," she whispered.

"But if I had, you wouldn't have been alone. I'd have done everything possible to comfort you."

"Could you have gotten rid of Renee?"

He was still for a moment, then he inhaled deeply. "What did she do to you?"

"Nothing."

"That's not true. You're scared of her."

"She…made me order things for her. She didn't have any money, so whenever my lawyer put cash in my account, she made me order treats and give them to her."

"She threatened you."

"Well, sure."

"Did she hurt you?"

"Not really. She…slapped me few times. After that, I did what she told me and kept out of her way. And she kept other women from bothering me."

He rubbed his cheek against her hair. "Laurel, you've been through so much. If I'd been part of your life back then, I'd probably have hired you a better lawyer."

His tender tone brought tears to her eyes. "Jim did all right. I guess."

"How can you say that? You almost got put away for life."

"I still could."

He held her tighter. "How did you survive with no one there to keep reminding you they loved you?"

She rested against his chest for a minute, soaking up the feel of him and the smell of him. "I prayed a lot." She lifted her head and peered at him intently. "You're the first person who's touched me since the murder—in a friendly way, I mean. The first person who really cared."

He pulled her back down against his shoulder. "You stay there as long as you want." He stroked her hair. "I read Renee's record. She was in for assault."

"Yeah. I didn't dare cross her. She got in trouble a few times for fighting. But it could have been worse for me, a lot worse."

"And the guards?"

"The female guards had to be tough. The men—well, I didn't have much contact with them."

They sat in silence, and Laurel went over the events in her mind. Bob's death, the investigation, her arrest and the agonizing wait of sixteen months before the trial.

She didn't want to think about the jail now, and the pain that went with it. She wanted to think about a bright future, perhaps one that would include Dan. He held her close, and she was comfortable in his arms. His soft breathing filled her with contentment, and she rested against him, deliciously warm.

There was one loose end that bothered her, and she sat up. "You never asked me."

"Asked you what?"

"If I did it."

"Ah, Laurel, why would I need to ask you that?" He tightened his arms around her.

She exhaled, feeling some of the weight lifted from her. "Pray for me, Danny."

"Of course."

"You ought to leave now."

"You're right." He stood up slowly. "I'll call later."

Knowing he would keep that simple promise encouraged her. She wasn't alone now.

SEVEN

Working in the empty office Monday night brought Laurel's anxiety to the forefront. After thirty nerve-racking minutes, she shoved the desk and chair around until she could see the doorway. Still, being alone in the large, open room with its bulky furniture and files casting deep shadows kept her on edge.

It was a relief when Troy came to check on things.

"I don't suppose you could come back in an hour and walk me to my car?"

Troy grinned. "My pleasure, Laurel."

Quickly she sought to erase any notion the security guard might have that she hoped to start a friendship.

"It's a little creepy out there."

He nodded. "Yeah, and now that the weather's warmer, the weirdos hang around later."

Laurel gritted her teeth and turned back to the monitor. "Thanks. I'll be ready around one o'clock."

When he came to escort her, she felt a little silly. But Dan's warnings simmered in the back of her mind, and she knew she shouldn't take chances. After all, her car had been burglarized right here in the parking lot.

"Beautiful night," Troy said as they climbed the concrete steps.

"Yes." She looked anxiously ahead, to where Judy's car was parked under a streetlight. She hoped nothing had happened to it. She hadn't wanted to drive it, but Judy insisted since the burglars knew her car. Dan had taken the Toyota to an undisclosed location. Best if she didn't know where, he'd said. A dealer would sell it without her ever seeing the middleman. If things went well, no one would recognize the name on the title, Laurel Wilson, and she would soon have enough money to buy another vehicle.

"Whoa, nice car." Troy appreciatively cased Judy's silver Lexus.

Laurel almost said, "Oh, it's not mine," but she bit that back. "Thanks."

It occurred to her that she stood out in Troy's mind for several reasons. If someone came around the hospital asking about her, Troy was an untapped source of information. Should she sound him out and ask him not to betray her? That in itself might be dangerous.

She unlocked the door, and Troy reached for the handle. "How come you need to work part-time nights, if you drive a car like this?"

She smiled at him. "Some folks spend it all on food and rent."

"Yeah, I get you. But you're not saying you live in a dump, are you? So you can have this car, I mean."

Laurel got into the driver's seat. "No, the place I'm staying in right now is not a dump. I'll see you, Troy."

"Hey." He caught the edge of the door before she could

swing it shut. "What do you say we go out sometime? Saturday night?"

She shook her head. "Thanks, but no. And thank you for walking me out here."

He stood watching her as she backed out of the parking slot. *The bumble factor,* Laurel thought. *He could give me away so easily. I can't him give any personal information. And warning him would only make him more curious.* Oh, yes, Troy would be fascinated by a mystery woman. She renewed her silent prayers for safety.

Dan watched the front windows of the house as he drove up Judy's driveway. He saw a flicker of movement at one. As his pickup eased toward the closed garage, the door began to rise. He drove in. Laurel stood in the doorway to the enclosed breezeway, and she lowered the overhead door as soon as his back bumper cleared it.

"Hi." He rounded the front of the pickup toward her. "I've got your stuff."

"Judy's not home," Laurel said. "She told me to have you park inside if you came."

He nodded. "Are you going crazy cooped up in there?"

"Not yet." She smiled. "I asked Judy if it would be safe to walk out back, and she said only if I had a big, brawny policeman with me."

"Let's go." Dan grinned and reached for her hand.

Laurel led him into the breezeway and out the patio door to the backyard. She locked the door, and in seconds they entered a leafy path that penetrated the patch of woods behind the house.

"Judy says this trail comes out behind a development. It's a green space, whatever that is."

"Gives the homeowners space and privacy, I guess. I'll unload your computer when we go back."

Dan wondered how far he could stretch his lunch hour and decided he'd better not waste time. He held back an aggressive maple branch for Laurel, and she ducked under it, smiling up at him with a trace of shyness.

"Thanks for coming."

"I should have come last night," he replied.

"No, you can't wear yourself out."

He stopped walking, and she did, too. When he looked down at her, he knew he hadn't been wrong. He felt certain about his feelings for her and his desire to help her. It wasn't just her beauty. He admired her strength and determination, despite her apparent fragility. He wanted to kiss her, but her brown eyes were shadowed with fatigue, and he reminded himself of their quest and his responsibility. *Not yet,* he told himself.

"I was a little uneasy last night," she confessed. "Judy didn't get home until late. One of her patients had an emergency."

"Did you get to work on time?"

"Yeah. Barely."

"I printed out all the stuff I could get on your case. I want more information, but I'll have to get my lieutenant or someone higher up to authorize it."

"Why? You already know how it turned out."

"I need to see all the reports, the court transcripts, the witness statements, the autopsy report…everything."

She reached toward him. "Dan, there's nothing you can

do to change the outcome now. If you're thinking you can, you're mistaken."

"But the judge could send you to trial again anytime."

She froze with her hand in midair, and he seized her fingers.

"Laurel, if that happens, I want to be ready. I don't want any surprises. And if there's something… Well, I don't want to give you false hope, but I've seen it happen before, where they think they have the right suspect so they quit looking at anyone else. If the investigators let something go by because they thought they had the murderer— like I said, it's happened before."

"My lawyer begged them to look at other people." She stared past him down the path toward where it opened on a long, narrow meadow.

"Was there anything at all that pointed to somebody else?"

"I don't know. I'm not sure they would have told me if there was." She frowned as she looked into his eyes. "I didn't count on this optimism."

He laughed. "A little hope doesn't hurt. So, you don't mind if I ask my lieutenant to help me on this?"

"I guess not."

He could almost read her mind. It would devastate her to believe he could help her and then be convicted of murder.

"Let's walk." He laced his fingers through hers and led her along the path toward the opening.

She chuckled, scuffing her sneakers on the grass. "Never thought I'd be holding hands with a cop."

"We're here to protect you, Laurel."

"I know." She shrugged. "When I was a little girl, I got the policemen-are-our-friends routine. But when I was arrested, I found out they're only your friends if they think you're innocent."

He eyed her sharply. "The Hatchers weren't your friends, either."

"No. When I took my maiden name back, part of me was glad. It put me one degree further away from Wayne and Renata. But it seemed disloyal to Bob, and I felt like Bob needed some true loyalty."

"As opposed to false loyalty?"

"Laugh if you want, but I couldn't help feeling his family mourned the loss of his business sense more than anything else."

"Your mother-in-law said you and Bob fought before the murder." Dan watched her closely, waiting for her reaction.

"Everybody fights once in a while."

"What did you fight over?"

"Her, mostly."

He smiled.

"It wasn't really fighting, but we talked a lot about how his family pulled us apart. Oh, look!" She dropped his hand suddenly and knelt by the path. She pushed back the leaves of a low-growing plant. "Isn't it beautiful?"

"Jack-in-the-pulpit?"

"Yes. We have them in Maine. They're shy, though." The subdued colors and the perfect curve of the foliage reminded him of the drawings he had seen in her sketchbook.

He pulled her up and into his arms. "How could anyone not believe you would stop to look at wildflowers on the way home from the store?"

She exhaled in surprise. "You read that?"

"Yes. It was so like you."

She leaned against him for just a moment, then pushed away gently, as though she was certain it would be a mistake to let his embrace become a habit.

"Ryan, 279." She traced his badge with her fingertip. "What's your middle name?"

An obvious ploy to change the subject, but that was all right; he would progress at her pace. "Daniel."

She raised her eyebrows.

"It's Michael Daniel Ryan. My father is Mike, so I'm Dan."

He touched her hair, tracing her rippling braid. "You're an only child?"

"Yes."

"How long have your folks been gone?"

"Too long. My mom died when I was eleven. Breast cancer. And my dad was killed in a fire when I was twenty. I was away at college." She shook her head. "I don't want to think about those times now."

"All right. Let's head back."

They walked along the path still holding hands. Laurel unlocked the patio door, and Dan secured it when they were inside.

"All right, Michael Daniel Ryan, Junior, you can flex your muscles and haul my computer in here while I microwave the leftovers."

"Fine." He chuckled. "Except I'm the fourth, not the second."

"The fourth? Oh, dear. That brings obligations."

They both laughed and sweet contentment flowed through him. For a while, they could forget that she was Laurel Wilson Hatcher, murder suspect. She needed an interlude of repose, a time to build trust and companionship. He wanted to give her that.

"Well, my grandpa was Dan and his father was Michael, so I guess the next generation gets saddled with Michael." He looked steadily into her rich, brown eyes.

"I'll try to remember which generation you are."

He smiled. "Danny is fine."

The color flamed in her cheeks, and he knew she remembered calling him Danny when she asked him to pray for her while he held her close. "I was a bit overwhelmed Sunday, I think."

"That's all right. When you're overwhelmed, you call me Danny. Otherwise, Dan will do."

Her blush deepened, and he laughed. He leaned down and brushed her cheek with a featherlight kiss, then headed for the garage.

"This woman lives in town?" Lieutenant Powers asked, scanning the printouts Dan had put in his hand when he'd returned from his lunch break.

"Yes, she's been here almost a month, but it just came through on our updates from the state police. She's staying with a friend on the north side of town, and she checks in with the Maine authorities once a week."

"Why didn't they notify us?"

"They did," Dan said. "We have it on file. And she has to report in person to the state police once a month. But she's not likely to commit a crime."

"You don't know that."

"Yes, I do."

Powers's eyes narrowed. "This is personal."

"Well, yes."

The lieutenant shook his head. "I don't like it, Ryan."

"What don't you like?"

"You getting mixed up in this."

"She's innocent," Dan insisted.

"That's what they all say."

"No, this is for real. She didn't do it."

"You have proof?" Powers asked.

"I wish. But I don't need proof to know it's true."

Powers sighed. "Big mistake, Ryan."

"I don't think so. Will you authorize some extra research for me?"

"What if I won't?"

"I'll ask the captain, and if he won't, I'll go to the chief."

"Stubborn, aren't you?"

"It's me Irish blood."

Powers snorted. "I want a report on my desk every day. I want to know what you're doing about this. Don't hold anything back."

"It's not an official case," Dan protested. "I just want to look it over, see if they missed anything."

"If you're looking at it, it's my business. I can be stubborn, too, laddie."

The files were so thick by five o'clock Wednesday that Dan put them into the soft briefcase he used to carry papers to the courthouse. He drove straight to Judy's house in the pouring rain.

Laurel greeted him with a smile. "Judy will be home soon."

Dan nodded. Regardless of her rap sheet and her four-year marriage, she possessed an innocence that tugged at him. "I brought everything. I hope it's not too intimidating." He set the briefcase on the coffee table.

She eyed it warily. "Come on. I'm making spaghetti."

They went through the dining room, where the table was set for three, with delicate, iris-sprigged white dishes. In the spacious kitchen, she went to the stove, lifted the lid on a kettle and stirred the sauce.

Dan watched her, glad just to be in the same room with her again. He wanted to give her hope, but it wouldn't be fair to have her hope if he couldn't deliver.

"Did you tell Judy about your case?"

"Not yet." She turned toward him, holding the wooden spoon out away from her clothing. "I really like her, but I didn't want to just dump it on her."

"We'll tell her over supper." He moved in closer to her.

"Do you really think we ought to?"

"Laurel, you live with her. I think she ought to know. You trust her, don't you?"

Her eyelashes flickered as he touched her shoulder. "Well, yes, but I hardly know her. I mean…what if she's upset and wants me to leave?"

"Then you go."

She swallowed. "I couldn't tell her that first night. It's too personal. And Monday night she was late and I had to go right to work."

"I know, and if things were going to continue as they are, I wouldn't push it. But if we're going to tear into this investigation and spend every waking minute trying to find a way to help you, she's got to know. It wouldn't be fair not to tell her."

Laurel looked deep into his eyes. "Is that what you intend to do? I'm…not sure it's worth it. What could we possibly find?"

"I don't know yet, but I couldn't live with myself if I don't give it everything I've got. I couldn't stand by and watch them take you off to jail again."

He slid his arm around her and their undeniable attraction crackled between them. Dan hoped she would give in to it and nestle down on his shoulder. If she would let him, he could comfort her and perhaps renew the faith she'd lost during her incarceration. Deep down, he believed he would find something that would sway a different jury.

But she stood stiff as she watched him. Was she thinking about the possibility of a life prison sentence? If she let him care for her the way he wanted to, what would happen when the verdict came in? Would she be torn from his arms in the courtroom?

He decided he'd better close the distance fast, before she followed the train of thought that far. He took the spoon from her hand, laid it on the edge of the range and gently pulled her toward him. Her dark eyes swam with emotion as her hands landed lightly on his shirt, just below his collarbone, and slid ever so slowly toward his shoulders. Everything in her seemed to soften, even as she tried to keep her resolve. Dan's heart pounded.

The garage door went up with a creak and a rattle, causing Laurel to jump back.

Judy appeared in the kitchen doorway. "It smells great in here."

"Hi." Dan stepped away from Laurel.

Judy's eyes widened in pleasure. "We have a guest tonight?"

"Yes." Laurel laughed. "I hope you like spaghetti, because I cooked too much, even with Dan here." He found it hard to look away from her blushing face.

"Just let me wash up, and I'll be right back," Judy said.

"Let me tell her," Laurel said, when Judy had left the kitchen. Avoiding his gaze, she grabbed the colander and put it in the sink to strain the spaghetti.

"All right." He leaned back against the counter. Clearly, there were still obstacles to overcome. There was Bob Hatcher's memory, and an uncertain future. Laurel was leery of commitment—even of caring—until she was free from the threat of life imprisonment. He'd checked the legal database to be sure Maine had no death penalty, but it was bad enough. She had reason to be cautious. Patience, he told himself.

Laurel waited until they were well into the meal, and Dan followed her lead, keeping the conversation on pleasant topics. She helped Judy clear the dishes and bring ice cream and coffee to the table. As she sat down again, Laurel turned to her hostess.

"Judy, Dan and I have something to tell you."

Judy took a sip of coffee and gave them her full attention. "I'm listening."

Laurel swallowed hard. "I'm on bail," she said quietly.

Judy stared at Laurel, obviously waiting for the punch line. There was none. She turned to Dan, her eyebrows drawn tightly together. "That's what this is about? All this secrecy? I mean, you told me Laurel was in danger, but…"

Dan flexed his shoulders. "She was accused of a crime two years ago. She went to court a few months back, and the judge declared a mistrial. There's a possibility they could recall her for another trial."

"Qh." Judy studied Laurel's face, then Dan's.

Laurel stared down at her melting ice cream. "If you don't want me to live here, I'll understand. I should have told you sooner, but—" She broke off and grabbed her napkin, chasing a tear with it.

Judy turned a quizzical look on Dan, her eyebrows arched and her lips parted.

"I think she's trying to say she didn't mean to deceive you," Dan explained. "It's just time you knew. Especially since Laurel and I are going to try to find some new evidence that will clear her."

"I guess I can cope with that." Judy picked up her spoon and took a bite of ice cream. "You didn't poison your last roommate, did you?"

Laurel began to giggle, and Judy laughed, too.

"So, tell me everything."

"Are you sure?" Laurel asked.

"Absolutely."

"In a nutshell, my husband was shot...and they thought I did it."

Judy kept on eating the ice cream in silence. When the ice cream was gone, she laid down her spoon.

"You're full of surprises. I had no idea you'd been married."

Laurel looked away, unsure of what to say.

Judy gazed at her compassionately. "You're not the only one with a gruesome past. I made a poor choice, and the guy turned out to be a real heel. He left me after fifteen years of marriage."

"Oh, Judy, I'm sorry."

She shrugged. "I was miserable at the time, but since then I've learned I can have a life again. And God—" her eyes grew softer "—God showed me He could take me as I was and make something worthwhile."

Laurel nodded gravely. "I hope someday I can have a life again. But until this mess is settled, everything is sort of dangling."

"So I take it you didn't kill him?"

"No," Laurel said with a faint smile. "Dan is hoping to find some new evidence, but…" She glanced toward him, then dropped her gaze. "I don't have a lot of expectations right now."

"You wouldn't kill him." Judy picked up her coffee cup. "Now I *felt* like killing Paul, but I restrained myself. His new wife can do that if she wants to."

Dan smiled and sipped his coffee. Judy was coming through for Laurel, as he'd hoped she would.

"I was wondering if you'd be interested in looking at the autopsy report from the homicide," he said. "I don't have much experience in medicine, and it's pretty technical."

Judy's brows went up. "I'd be honored. That is, if Laurel doesn't mind."

Tears welled in Laurel's eyes and spilled over. "I can't believe you want to get involved in this. First Dan, now you."

"I love mysteries. Bring it on."

Dan got up to retrieve the briefcase.

For two hours they sat at the table, going over the data he had collected. Judy read the autopsy report with interest and explained some of the medical terms, but she found nothing that contradicted the court testimony given by the medical examiner. The time of death was placed at between 1:00 and 2:00 p.m., the last hour before Laurel said she had arrived home.

The story caught Judy's interest, and she read the clippings and police reports avidly. Laurel hesitated, but then she, too, began to examine the papers.

"It's like it happened to somebody else," she said at last. "They were so sure I did it, and no one would listen to me. Reading this stuff, I'm beginning to understand why. If I hadn't been there, I'd probably believe I did it, too."

"There's got to be more," Dan insisted. "We've got your statement to the police, but there had to be other witnesses they questioned. I mean, it says right here—" he held up the thick court transcript and pointed "—the officers questioned all the close neighbors and came up with nothing. I want to see the original reports they made when they did that questioning."

He tossed the transcript onto the table and stood up to pace. "I wonder what would happen if I called this investigator with the Maine State Police, Lieutenant Dryer. I don't want to stir things up if it won't help, but I want to know if they're still looking for clues, or if they've stuffed this thing in a file cabinet and forgotten about it."

"You could talk to my lawyer," Laurel suggested.

"Good idea," Dan said.

"Laurel will have to talk to the attorney and authorize him to discuss the case with you," Judy pointed out.

"Are you willing to do that?" Dan asked.

Laurel shrugged. "Sure. But I doubt it will do any good."

"It would be a start," Dan said.

Laurel glanced at her watch. "I have to leave for work now. I could call him tomorrow."

"Great. Call me when you've talked to him." Dan began to gather up the papers. "By the way, your car was sold today. I'll pick up your check tomorrow."

"Should I buy another one?"

He shook his head. "Better wait and see what develops."

"I don't mind if you use mine in the evenings a little longer," Judy said.

"Thanks so much," Laurel told her. "For everything, Judy. I didn't know how you'd react when you heard the whole story."

Judy smiled. "You kind of threw me in the ocean with my clothes on, but if there's any way I can help, just tell me."

Laurel nodded soberly.

"They should let you work at home soon, anyway," Judy said. "I spoke to the CEO about it yesterday."

Dan closed the briefcase. "Come on, Laurel. I'll walk you to the car."

They went out into the garage, and Laurel stopped next to Judy's car.

"Thank you, Dan."

"We've got to find something, that's all." He stroked her glossy hair.

"If God wills," she whispered.

"How could He want you to go to prison?"

"I don't know, but it has happened to innocent people before."

Dan shuddered. "I don't want to stir things up and make

them decide to send you back to trial unless we find something positive."

"I know. But anything would be better than just waiting. I can't go on indefinitely, knowing they could call me any day. I can't move on with my life, Dan. Do you understand?"

He took a deep, ragged breath. She was pleading with him to realize she couldn't fall in love with him, couldn't share a life with him, knowing it might be shattered in an instant. He held her look, but the ache in his chest intensified. "You've agreed to let me try to help you."

"I shouldn't have. It wasn't fair."

"It's too late, sweetheart." He pulled her against him, and just for a moment she let him hold her. Then she pushed away and got in the car. He stood looking after her as she drove away.

EIGHT

"He's a police officer," Laurel told her attorney on the phone the next morning.

"In Ohio."

"Yes."

"Ohio cops have no jurisdiction here, Laurel," Jim Hight said.

"I know that. And he knows that. He just wants to go over the records and see if anything was overlooked during the original investigation."

"I did everything I could."

"I know you did. I'm not suggesting otherwise," Laurel said softly.

"If some cop starts poking around, someone in Augusta might remember that the prime suspect in this case is walking free."

Laurel held her ground. "Jim, a few months ago you told me you believed I was innocent. I want to be done with this. I want a new life, and I can't have that unless the case is resolved."

He sighed. "You probably won't have to wait much longer. They can't put this off forever, and I expect to hear from the court any day. Does this guy have a private investigator's license in Ohio?"

"I don't think so."

"Well, if he had one and you hired him as a P.I., it might be useful. He could do some work on this end, get at some records and things."

"He can't just get them as a police officer?"

"If for some reason the Ohio police were investigating you, yes, but there's no reason for that. Is there?"

"Of course not," she snapped.

"Okay. I'll give Ryan what we have, but I doubt he'll get very far with the state police. If he's not officially investigating…you see what I mean? I'm surprised he's already got as much data as you tell me he's got."

Not truly satisfied, Laurel called Dan at the police station.

"Don't be upset," he counseled. "I've been praying all morning that he'd just be willing to talk to me. It's a start. And I'll ask Lieutenant Powers about applying for a P.I.'s license. I'm sure I could get one, but it would take time. Maybe he could cut through some red tape for me."

"You think Jim is right, that you'd have more access as a P.I. than as a police officer?"

"Not more access, but anonymity. I don't want to draw attention to your case at this point."

Dan had several conversations with Jim Hight over the next few days, and the lawyer mailed him a packet of photocopied documents. There wasn't anything there that Dan didn't know already, and Hight seemed a little disgruntled that Laurel had turned to him for support. Dan called him again on his lunch hour on Friday.

"We put on a good defense," Hight said stiffly, his pride clearly hurt.

"I read the transcript."

"You think we could have done more?"

"I don't know," Dan admitted. "I wasn't there. It seems to me you made all the pertinent points, based on what you had to work with. But I can't help wondering if there was more that you never got a chance to work with."

"Such as?"

"Interviews with neighbors. Clues. Anything that would point to someone else. Once they settled on Laurel as their target, the prosecution ignored everything else."

"And just what is *everything else?*" Hight asked. "I followed up every single lead."

"What were some of them?" Dan asked.

"It's all in what I sent you. A kid at the golf course said Bob took a call during the golf match. I spent some time on that. Turns out his father called him about something connected with work."

"Yes, I saw that."

"The golf game ended early, so I interviewed Bob's golf buddy. The guy had a headache, so they called it an early day."

"There's got to be something else," Dan insisted.

"If there is, it never got to my office. I had the trial postponed last year, and again this spring, hoping for a break, but…"

Dan sighed.

"Look, if you can turn up something new, I'd love to hear it," Hight said. "I believe in Laurel, but she made it difficult to defend her. She was pretty shell-shocked when it happened. I still believe that was because she loved her husband. Jail was tough on her, too. I don't have anything new that will help her case, though."

"I have to try," Dan said resolutely.

"Well, if it's that way, of course. I'll do anything I can on this end."

Dan felt slightly better about Laurel's choice of lawyers, but he knew it was up to him alone to find the crucial evidence they needed.

By the weekend, Laurel had accepted Dan's tenacity. He had attended the string quartet's two rehearsals, but had warned the others that he needed a hiatus from their rigorous schedule after Saturday's benefit concert.

"He committed to the concert with the rest of us a long time ago," Judy told her as they cleaned up the kitchen Friday evening. "We'll be helping raise money for the community college's music program. But I'd say Dan's found a critical cause now."

"I don't want to take him away from his music," Laurel said.

Judy smiled. "I don't think you have a choice. He's decided to put all his energy into your case, so the quartet will have to work around that."

"Can I go to the concert?"

"If Dan thinks it's safe. I'd love for you to meet the others."

Laurel nodded pensively. It might be her only chance to hear Dan play with the quartet.

Judy poured the soap into the dishwasher. "Dan seems to be spending all his lunch hours and evenings on your case."

"Sometimes I feel helpless," Laurel said. "I want to

help him find something, so I answer his questions and read through reams of reports. But I don't know what we're looking for, and I think after a while he'll do what my lawyer did and give up looking."

"Be patient. It's a labor of love for him."

Laurel grasped Judy's arm. "I can't encourage him too much right now. If nothing comes of all his hard work, I can't allow him to get too attached." She picked up the dishcloth and scrubbed at the counter that was already clean. Judy watched her in silence. At last she tossed the cloth into the sink. "It would be so easy."

"What would?" Judy asked.

"To love him. But I can't," Laurel replied.

"I would laugh at you, but this isn't funny."

Laurel bit her lip as tears filled her eyes. "No, it's not funny at all."

"This thing about you and Bob fighting," Dan said on Saturday morning. "We need to talk about it."

They sat in lawn chairs on Judy's patio. Dan had scouted the neighborhood first, to be sure there were no strangers lurking about. Laurel felt lazy in the warm sunshine. She kicked off her sandals and stretched out in the chaise lounge. Judy sat nearby, leafing through a medical journal while Dan pulled files out of the briefcase.

"What do you want to know?" Little white clouds scudded about high in the sky. Laurel would rather think about anything other than the Hatcher family.

"How did you meet Bob?" Dan asked.

Judy laid the medical journal on her lap and made no pretense of disinterest.

"At school," Laurel said.

"Tell me more."

It's for the investigation, she told herself. *He has to know everything, even if it has no bearing on the case.*

"We met through a Christian organization on campus. They held Bible studies and sponsored activities." She looked over at Dan, and he gestured for her to continue. "Bob started coming to the Bible study with his roommate. He asked the group to pray for him because he had to decide whether to go to work for his father after graduation or cut loose from the family business. I put him on my prayer list and kept praying for him for weeks. He kept coming to the group. I could see that he was interested in me, but I tried not to encourage him. Until one day—"

"What?"

The memories of those days deluged her. "His friend told me Bob wanted to take me to a play, but was too shy to ask me. Then I…"

"Quit not encouraging him?" Judy asked with one raised eyebrow.

"Well, yes."

"Was Bob Hatcher an honest man?" Dan asked.

"What?" She tried to suppress the annoyance his question raised.

"It may be important to the case. Was Bob honest? And was he a true Christian?"

"No doubt about that. He went against his family and everything he'd been taught."

"Tell me about that." Dan's voice was gentler.

She thought back to that time, trying to be objective. "Well, the Hatchers aren't billionaires, but they own

Hatcher & Brody Construction and it's a thriving business."

"What do they build?" Judy asked.

"Big bridges, a couple of dams, some substantial buildings, even some highway sections. Right now they're building a prison in upstate New York."

"But they weren't religious," Dan said.

"No, definitely not. And when Bob started going to church and talking about the Lord, his mother was furious. To her, religion is a social accessory."

"What about his father?"

"Wayne was easier to get along with. He ignored spiritual matters. Whatever made Bob happy was okay with him, as long as Bob stayed with Hatcher & Brody and brought projects in under bid."

"So Bob decided to go into the firm when he graduated." Dan shuffled the papers in one file. "He earned an engineering degree from the University of Maine."

"Right."

"When did you meet the family?"

"That summer. When school got out, Bob took me home for a weekend. His mother hated me from the start."

"Why?"

Laurel squirmed a little. "I don't want to say jealousy, but I think it was difficult for her to lose her son's attention to another woman. Of course, I wasn't in their social class, and my folks were dead. Renata sort of looked down her nose at me, like Bob had brought home a filthy little orphan."

"And Wayne?"

Laurel shrugged. "We got along better, but I was never really part of the family, except in Bob's eyes."

"And you were married the summer after you graduated." Dan scanned a sheaf of papers. "Who's the Brody in Hatcher & Brody?"

"Bob's Uncle Jack."

"His mother's brother?"

"Yes."

"Which brings us back to Renata Hatcher, the dragon lady."

"She was furious when Bob announced our engagement."

"That must have been rough on you."

"She tried to break us up. She bribed him and threatened him. Threw other girls at him every time he went home for a weekend."

"Why?" Judy asked, sitting up.

Those old feelings of inadequacy struck Laurel, and she drooped in her chair. "Renata hated everything about me. I majored in anthropology, which she considered to be a worthless field of study. Not only that, I had the gall never to use my degree. Instead I married her son and, in her view, sponged off his family. I painted mediocre acrylics. She bought old masters. I put up a badminton net in our yard. She played golf at the country club." She grimaced at Dan. "It was more than that, though. I was too conservative. And Bob wouldn't go along with a lot of things his family did after he became a Christian. I think she blamed me for that."

Dan sat forward eagerly. "What kind of things?"

"Well, he wouldn't drink anymore, even at client dinner parties, and Renata found that humiliating for some reason. And he wouldn't fudge figures on estimates. He gave his father a lot of headaches that way. Wayne decided he could live with it, if that's what it took to keep his straight-arrow son in the firm, but Renata wanted the old Bob back."

"You loved him," said Judy.

Laurel sank back into her chair and didn't look at Dan. "Of course. Bob was my hero. He stuck to his faith, even though his family derided him. He married me against their wishes and made his mother throw us a huge wedding. I think she was afraid people would think she was cheap if they let us elope. It was scary, but I figured he'd always be there as a buffer for me, and that once they got to know me, they'd resent me less. I think Wayne got to where he liked me a little. But not Renata."

"What about Bob's work situation?" Dan asked.

"He told his parents and Uncle Jack he was going to do things by the book, and if they didn't like it, he'd go work for someone else. I was so proud of him. The only thing was, they got him to stay. I hoped for a while that he'd actually go with one of their competitors."

"Was anyone angry enough to kill him?" Judy asked.

"Oh, no, they loved him, in their twisted way. Besides, this was back when we first got married. If they were angry enough to kill him then, why wait four years?"

"Something must have happened to turn somebody against him," Judy persisted.

"Someone hated him," Dan agreed. "They ruled out robbery at the murder scene."

"Yes. There was no evidence of a break-in, either."

"It says here there were no doors or windows left unlocked that day." Dan tapped the papers in his hand.

"The police said so. I didn't check."

"So nobody could have gotten in there unless Bob let them in."

Laurel shrugged. "I've thought about it, and I don't see how."

"Okay, it was Saturday. Bob played golf that morning."

"Yes, with his friend Larry."

"Oh, yes, Larry." Dan smiled grimly. "Bob's best friend, who did his best to put you away for life."

"It wasn't like that."

"Sounds like it to me." Dan flipped through the court transcript. "Here it is, right here. 'Laurel could beat me any day with a handgun. Prosecutor: Did you ever see Mrs. Hatcher fire her husband's nine-millimeter pistol? L. Mason: Yes, she and Bob were target shooting with it in the fall, before the murder. She knew how to handle it.'"

"But that's all true." Laurel remembered the day Larry went with them to practice at the shooting range Bob had set up in a gravel pit. "We shot a lot of cans and targets that day. Larry's pretty good. Not as good as Bob was."

"Not as good as you, either, apparently," Dan said.

She closed her eyes. She didn't like to think Larry believed she had killed Bob. He'd always been friendly to her. He and his wife, Tina, socialized with her and Bob.

"So they played golf that morning," Dan went on.

"Right. They played fairly often. I didn't think Bob would get home until late afternoon, and I went shopping."

"But he beat you home. His car was in the garage when you got there?"

"Yes."

"That would be the Corvette."

"Yes. Does it matter? Larry drove that day." Dan's tone

irritated her. He sounded a little too much like the state prosecutor. "Is there a problem? Other than my husband being murdered, I mean?"

He winced. "No. I'm sorry. Let's get back to what your mother-in-law said about the arguments."

She leaned back in the chair, regretting her hasty words. "Renata hated me. She'd ask Bob to do things with her and not include me. I tried to laugh it off, but it hurt. He spoke to her about it, and for a while things were better, but not much."

"So you had a fight?"

Laurel sighed. "I wouldn't have called it a fight. But I got careless and said something I shouldn't have in front of his mother. She grabbed it like a frog going for a fly. Used it to prove that I hated Bob's family, had no respect for my elders and didn't appreciate anything the Hatchers had done for us." She shook her head. "I prayed and cried over that. I'd tried to be careful and never give her a reason to criticize. As long as she hated me for no reason, I could bear it. But when I'd actually committed an offense, I couldn't defend myself."

Judy stood and collapsed her lawn chair.

"I need to get ready for the concert. You'd better get moving, Dan. Or have you got your tux in your pickup?"

"Afraid not. Guess I'd better go. I'll pick you both up in an hour."

Laurel's heart surged, but Judy laughed. "In your truck with two instruments? No thanks. We'll meet you at the hall. You can bring Laurel home if you want."

Laurel walked with Dan through the breezeway to the garage.

"Dan, is there something about the Corvette? You seemed to bridle at that."

He gave her a sheepish smile. "No. I don't have a problem with the Corvette. It's just…I was feeling a little jealous, I guess."

"Because of Bob's car?"

"No, silly. His wife."

NINE

The string quartet was scheduled to perform after several other artists in the concert. Laurel sat by herself in the second row at the community college auditorium, nervously waiting for Dan, Judy and their friends to come onstage. An a cappella choir, a solo pianist and a jazz guitarist came first. She sank back in her chair, relaxing as the melodies filled the hall.

She had seen Judy's black gown, and Dan had met them at the stage door when they arrived, so she was prepared for the group's formal attire. Dan in a tuxedo had taken a moment to assimilate. His friend Joe, the cellist, laughed at her expression.

"Hey, Daniel, hasn't this gal ever seen you in anything but a uniform?"

Laurel had blushed and stammered, but Dan didn't seem embarrassed when he introduced Joe and Marcia. She wondered if she should have worn something more formal herself, but when she went to join the audience, she found herself surrounded by teenagers in jeans and families in casual attire. Her print skirt and corduroy vest were a bit dressier than what most of the audience wore.

The quartet was announced, and Laurel held her breath.

They were beautiful, all four of them, and their music almost painfully perfect. Judy especially impressed Laurel with her skill in Beethoven's "Opus 18 No. 5."

Mozart's "Eine Klein Nacht Music" was one of Laurel's favorite pieces, and the entire ensemble played brilliantly, with the notes leaping out, fresh and bright.

As she watched Dan's face, a deep longing grew inside her. She wanted to understand this part of him. He focused intently on the music during those few minutes. He wasn't as proficient as Judy, but he was very good. She wondered how old he had been when he first held the bow in his hand. Only an excellent musician could keep up the tempo they maintained on the Beethoven piece.

The quartet received a thunderous ovation from the crowd, and she wondered if they would play an encore, but the master of ceremonies moved along smoothly to the next act, a vocal duet. Laurel wished she were backstage with Dan and the others. As the applause for the singers began, Dan slipped in beside her.

Laurel sat back, enjoying just being with him. The rest of the program whizzed by, and suddenly the emcee was thanking the audience and the performers.

Judy pushed through the crowd to the end of their row. "Marcia, Joe and I are going for coffee. Want to come?"

"Do you think it's safe?" Laurel asked as they edged into the aisle.

"We'd probably better skip it," Dan said. "Sorry. We took a chance letting you come here."

Judy nodded. "Okay, next time. You'll take care of Laurel?"

"Of course."

* * *

Dan drove at a leisurely pace, hating to arrive at Judy's house because that would mean he had to go home to change for his security shift at the hospital. He had a half hour to spare, and he intended to make the most of it.

He turned onto the main road that led north and reached for Laurel's hand.

She smiled at him. "I have some good news. The hospital is going to let me work at home. Judy fixed it as promised. I can pick up the pictures and hard copy anytime during the day and take it home to work on."

"Fantastic!" At least one thing was going right for her.

"You have to work again tonight, don't you?" Her brow wrinkled. "You look tired. Drop me off at Judy's and go take a nap."

"There's no time. But I have more questions for you." He paused. "There's something significant out there, Laurel. We just don't know what it is yet."

She took a deep breath. "All right, then. Fire away."

"When did Bob get the Corvette?"

"About four months before he died."

"Who paid for it?"

"Uncle Jack."

"Jack Brody."

"Yes. It was a gift."

"And Uncle Jack made a habit of giving Bob expensive gifts?"

"No." Her brown eyes were troubled. "That bothered me a little at the time."

"Why?"

"As you suggest, it was unusual. Jack said it was

because Bob was doing such a terrific job, but I wondered if it was supposed to be a…"

"A bribe?"

Laurel ducked her head. "Bob wouldn't be bribed. His mother tried that."

"Seriously?"

"At one point his dad wanted him to sign off on a bid that couldn't be executed without using substandard materials. Bob wouldn't do it. His mother figured she could change his mind and dangled a big bonus in front of him. But Bob told them he was ready to quit before he'd do anything underhanded. They lost the bid."

Dan sighed. "Okay, forget that angle." He saw a deep bereavement in her eyes and knew he had put that look on her face. "Laurel, I'm sorry."

She shook her head. "You have to ask me these things. I understand."

"I wish I knew if it was worth it." He squeezed her hand. "I don't want to make you dredge up painful memories. But if there's any way to help you—"

"It's worth it," she said. "As long as we keep at it, I have hope. Besides, I get to be with you." She smiled then, the heart-stopping smile that had captivated him the first time he saw her. "So, what other personal questions do you have for me?"

He signaled for his exit and looked over at her. She was so beautiful—her thick hair rippling over her shoulders, her deep brown eyes that penetrated into his heart.

His resolution to keep things in low gear was long gone, but he didn't care. He would use all his strength to clear her name. In his mind he was starting to see a future for them, full of sunlight and green meadows and laughing children.

He decided to go for the question that had been haunting him. "Why didn't you have any kids?"

She locked her hands together and sat looking out the window, silent for a long moment. "We planned to," she said finally. "Bob thought we should wait a couple of years. We were young. He wanted to get firmly established in his career."

"So, it was Bob's choice?"

She shrugged slightly. "I suppose so. We made the decision together, but it was his preference."

"If it had been up to you?"

"It doesn't matter."

"It matters to me," he said gruffly.

She seemed to struggle with the answer, and he regretted putting her on the spot.

"Sorry. Forget I asked."

"No. It was high on my list. But…we didn't fight about it, if you're wondering."

"I wasn't."

"I just felt I needed to defer to him in that, at least for the time being. Children were part of his plan, just not the immediate part." Her voice caught. "We did things Bob's way, and I don't regret that. I would have loved to have a child, but now I'm grateful we didn't. I shudder to think what would have happened when I was in jail. I had no family. Renata would probably have had custody." She leaned toward him, her eyes gleaming with a ferocity he'd never seen in her before. "I still want children someday."

"I hope God gives them to you." His throat felt tight as he flipped on his turn signal. Judy's house was dark, and he eased the pickup up to the garage door. Laurel raised the remote opener Judy had entrusted to her and pushed the button. As the door slid up, the headlights illuminated the interior of the garage.

"Judy should have left the light on." Dan pulled the pickup inside, and Laurel hit the button on the remote once more, to lower the overhead door. As he slipped the gearshift into Park and reached for the ignition, a sudden movement to the side startled him and a rush of adrenaline hit him. A dark-clad man stood beside his door.

Laurel gasped and Dan sensed without looking that a second figure had edged in past the rear bumper on the other side. He stayed his hand and left the engine idling.

"Get out," a man in a knit ski mask ordered, pointing his Glock at Dan's face from the other side of the glass.

"Laurel, don't move," Dan said.

He heard her labored breath, but she said nothing.

"What do you want?" Dan called. He hadn't opened the door yet, springing the locks.

"Get out!" the man demanded.

Glittering eyes showed through round eyeholes in the mask. Without moving his lips, Dan said softly, "Laurel, when I tell you, get down."

He heard the second man yanking at the door handle on Laurel's side. Dan reached slowly toward the gearshift.

The man beside him whacked the butt of his pistol against Dan's window. "I said now!"

"Get down!" Dan ducked as he shifted into Reverse. He felt Laurel dive and heard the explosion of the Glock's load as the side window shattered. Glass sprayed over his arm. *God, help us.*

He stood on the gas pedal and they roared back, smashing through the garage door and dragging a large panel down the driveway. He whipped the truck around on the lawn and shoved the lever into Drive. A bullet pinged against metal, but he didn't think it entered the cab. He straightened the wheel and gunned it down Judy's street.

"Laurel?"

She stirred and he glanced over in the darkness. She was huddled on the floor, bracing herself between the passenger seat and the dashboard.

"You okay?"

"Yeah."

"Stay there for now." In the rearview mirror he saw headlights in the distance behind them. He fumbled in the pocket of his tux for his phone and tossed it onto Laurel's seat. "Can you call 911?"

A moment later, the dim light illuminated her face as she frowned over the miniature keypad.

"Give it to me when it rings," Dan said.

Seconds later, she thrust it into his outstretched hand. "This is Patrol Officer Dan Ryan. I'm off duty, and I was just ambushed and shot at while attempting to visit a friend on Peachtree Lane." He gave the dispatcher the details of the attack while driving steadily toward town. His intentions formed in his mind as he spoke. "I'm heading south, and I'll come to the police station soon. I don't think I'm being followed, but I need to hang up so I can concentrate on my driving."

Laurel stayed curled on the floor, and he handed her the phone.

"Call Judy. Tell her not to go home. I'll call her again once I know you're safe."

Laurel's voice trembled as she assured Judy that they were all right and the police were on the way to Judy's house. A few minutes later, Dan slowed for a turn.

"You can get up now. I'm sorry you had to go through this."

She pulled herself onto the seat and looked around. "We're headed for the police station?"

"I need to go in and make a statement."

"You didn't tell them I was with you."

Dan gritted his teeth, hoping he wasn't making the wrong decision. "We'll make a short stop first." He glanced over at her. The killers were desperate enough to attack Laurel in her home. He needed to take her to a place where they couldn't find her. *Lord, give me wisdom.*

Dan banged on the door, trying to think of a better solution as he waited. Laurel stood shivering next to him, keeping her face averted from the street.

At last the door swung open, and Terry Wyman stood before them with a sleepy, baffled expression. He was barefoot, wearing cutoffs and a T-shirt.

"Dan. What's up?"

"I'm sorry, Terry. I know it's late, but we need your help."

Terry blinked. "Sure."

"Can Laurel stay here tonight?"

He was wide-awake now, squinting at Laurel. "Is something wrong?"

"Yes. Can we come in, please? I'll explain."

"Sure. I'll tell Donna."

As they entered the living room, Donna joined them, wearing her housecoat and slippers. She smiled uncertainly at Dan. "Hi. Nice threads."

Dan smiled back. He'd forgotten about his tuxedo. When he looked down, he noticed a tear in the left sleeve and wondered if it was ruined. A trickle of blood smeared across the back of his hand and stained the cuff of his white shirt. "Thanks."

"Laurel needs a bed for the night," Terry said.

Donna's eyebrows shot up. "I guess we can arrange that."

"I'm really sorry." Dan hesitated. *What am I asking of my friends?*

"Got luggage?" Terry asked.

Laurel shook her head and looked at Dan. "This is probably not a good idea."

"I don't know what else to do," Dan said. "It's here or the station."

"Let's put the coffeepot on and talk," Donna suggested.

"I don't have time," Dan told her. "We'll give you the short version, and if you don't want to be in the middle of it, I won't blame you. But I need to make a phone call first."

"Come on, Laurel." Donna reached toward her. "Help me out in the kitchen."

Dan took out his phone. "Shut the curtains."

Donna stared at him, then nodded.

"Are you calling Judy again?" Laurel asked.

"Yeah. I'm going to suggest she stay with Marcia tonight, but the police will want to talk to her."

He dreaded telling Judy what he'd done to her garage

door. She made light of it, showing much more concern for him and Laurel than for her house. Dan insisted she not stay there until the garage was secured.

"And if your homeowner's insurance won't pay for the damage, you tell me. My dad and I will fix it ourselves."

Terry lingered while he made the call, then took him to the kitchen, where Donna had Laurel seated at the table drinking strong coffee.

"I guess it's time for explanations," Dan said. "And I'm serious. If you want us to leave, we will."

"Laurel's been telling me about it. A home invasion." Donna shook her head.

"Yeah. Two thugs slipped into the garage behind us when we drove in." Dan flogged himself mentally. He should have been more alert. "So...did she tell you the rest?"

"You mean about her trial?" Donna asked. "She just told me."

Terry arched his eyebrows.

"Tell you later, babe," Donna said.

Dan sipped the coffee she had placed before him and felt drained of his strength.

"What happened to your hand?" Terry asked.

Dan looked down. The cut had stopped bleeding, and the blood had congealed. "I guess a piece of glass got me. It's not serious." He looked at Terry and Donna. "So...can I leave Laurel here while I go over to the station and make my statement? I want them to catch these guys, but I need to leave Laurel out of it."

Terry's jaw dropped. "You're just going to lie to the department and tell them she wasn't with you?"

Dan felt his face flush. "No, I'm just going to…not tell them she *was* with me."

Donna brought him a clean, wet dishcloth. "Dan, this isn't right."

He swabbed at his wound, not meeting her eyes, and flicked the shard of glass from the skin on his hand. "Laurel doesn't want to go to the police station."

"Danny, I think we're beyond that." Laurel's voice trembled. "I was wrong not to listen to you before."

He searched her face. "Are you sure?"

Laurel nodded.

"Let's pray," Donna said.

Dan swallowed hard. "Yeah. Okay."

Laurel's hands shook as she set her mug down. She reached hesitantly toward him, and he gripped her hand.

Donna sat down beside Terry, and he began to pray. "Lord, thank You for letting Donna and me be here when Dan and Laurel needed help. Please help them to make a wise decision here—Your decision. Let them want what You want."

When Terry was finished, Dan gazed over at Laurel, whose eyes were bright with unshed tears. He knew that he'd do anything to protect her, including risking his life to safeguard hers.

"We'll wait up for you," Donna said. "Come back when you're finished. I'll have a bed made up for Laurel."

"I'm ready to go with you, Danny," Laurel said.

He nodded. "Okay. Let's go give the police what they need to catch those guys. Whatever it takes."

TEN

"I'll have to call Augusta first thing tomorrow and tell my probation officer where I am," Laurel told Dan the next morning. Terry and Donna had left for church, but Dan refused to risk letting Laurel be seen in public again.

He nodded. "Don't use Terry's phone to call. You can use my cell phone, or I'll take you to a pay phone. That might be best."

Laurel bit her lip. "I'm afraid for Terry and Donna. Look at what happened at Judy's."

"I know. I've been thinking about it, too. We can't keep asking our friends to take risks for us."

"Your friends," she corrected him. "They don't know me. I'm only here because they trust you."

"They'll know you better when this is over, and they'll be glad they helped." He rubbed his jaw and his aching neck. He'd have to quit the hospital job. Sleep deprivation could result in disaster. He needed to be in top form to shield Laurel from harm. Sighing, he leaned back in Terry's armchair.

"I can't stay here." Laurel sat rigid on the edge of the sofa and squeezed her hands together. "I'm glad the police let us go last night. I was afraid they'd make me stay at the station."

"They had no reason to hold you. Laurel, I—"

"What?"

Her eyes were bloodshot, and he knew she hadn't slept much more than he had. "I'm sorry about last night."

"It's not your fault," she said. "From the very first, you wanted me to keep the police involved but I let fear override my common sense. I was wrong not to report it when Renee broke into the apartment. I just hope it's not too late for them to intervene."

He rubbed a hand over his scratchy face. Shaving was now a time-consuming luxury. "I'm glad they didn't put you in protective custody. We need to keep you free so we can find the evidence."

"Do you really believe I have something—or know something—that will clear me?"

"Someone believes it."

Her shoulders sagged. "I'm a hazard to anyone who associates with me. This has to stop."

"You're right—we can't keep putting others in danger." He paused. "You should quit your job."

She blinked at him. "So soon?"

"They must have traced you through the hospital and followed Judy's car to her house. That's the only place they could have made the connection."

Her mouth felt dry. "Troy. I wondered if he'd spill it."

"It could have been him, or some well-meaning clerk in personnel. The men who attacked us probably waited there for you to come in, then followed you."

Her lips trembled as she inhaled. "I'm scared, Danny. They know you're helping me now, and they may follow you."

"I borrowed an unmarked car from the police department's motor pool until my truck window is fixed."

"That's good. Still, Terry and Donna could be the next victims. We've got to leave."

He stared across the room for several seconds. "I'll give my notice at the hospital tonight. You're right. We need to burn some bridges."

Early Monday morning Laurel met Dan at the Wymans' door when he stopped there before reporting for duty at the police station. Dark smudges beneath his eyes betrayed his fatigue. At Terry and Donna's insistence, Laurel had reluctantly agreed to stay with them one more night, giving Dan time to make other arrangements, and the hours had passed without incident.

"You look awful."

"Oh, thanks." His smile etched fine lines at the corners of his mouth.

"Did you give notice at the hospital?"

"I'm all done there."

She winced but refrained from commenting on the bad things her case had brought into his life. He gave her his phone, and she punched in Mr. Webster's number with shaking fingers.

"Mrs. Hatcher! I was going to call you."

"You were?" Webster's words fanned the dread that always smoldered in her chest. "I've moved again, Mr. Webster."

"Oh? Let me take the new address. Not having problems, I hope?"

"I…" Laurel gulped. "Why were you going to call me, sir?"

"I have news for you."

She looked at Dan, and he gave her a sympathetic smile.

"The superior court judge has set a date for a new trial."

A lump formed in her throat.

"Did you hear me, Mrs. Hatcher?"

"Yes, sir."

"The date is June nineteenth. You will report to Augusta Superior Court that morning at eight o'clock."

"Y-yes, eight o'clock."

"That's right. Now, what is your new address?"

Dan had already coached her to give his own cell phone number and home address. She didn't like it, and she knew Dan didn't, either, but it was the only recourse to avoid putting his loved ones at risk.

"All right," Webster said. "Good luck."

"Wait!"

Laurel was afraid he'd hung up, but he asked patiently, "What is it?"

"Why?"

"I beg your pardon?"

"Why the new trial?" she demanded. "Is there new evidence? I haven't heard a thing!"

"I don't have that information," Webster said. "Perhaps your attorney could advise you."

"Thank you." She tried to close the phone, fumbled with it and handed it to Dan.

"Are you all right?" he asked.

"The trial." Her voice was hoarse.

"When?"

"June nineteenth."

She sat on the couch and leaned back, closing her eyes. She knew the jury would be strictly charged to reach a verdict this time. The state would not want the expense of a third trial. One way or another, the rest of her life would be determined.

She felt Dan's strong arm around her shoulders, and she opened her eyes.

"I'm here," he whispered.

She leaned against his shoulder. "It's only a month away."

"That's not much time. We'd better call your lawyer. And you need to quit your job today, Laurel. Don't go to the hospital again."

She nodded.

Donna came to the kitchen doorway carrying her three-year-old daughter. "Can I get you some coffee, Dan?"

"No, thanks. I've got to get to work." He stood up. "We just found out Laurel's trial date has been set."

"That's good, right?" Donna asked.

He shrugged. "Maybe. I'll call Jim Hight from the police station, Laurel. And, Donna, I'll move her soon."

"We don't mind if she stays a while longer, Dan. Really."

"No, we've been over that. I'm moving her tonight."

"We'll be praying for you," Donna said.

Laurel walked with him to the door, wishing he could stay and finalize their plans.

"I'm going with you," Dan said.

"Tonight?"

"To Maine. To the trial."

She caught her breath. "Do you think that's wise?"

"Yes. I've got three weeks' vacation. Might be able to stretch it to four, without pay the last week."

His generosity went beyond her wildest hopes. Having him beside her when she entered the courthouse again, knowing he was nearby while she waited for the proceedings to begin, seeing him in the courtroom as she faced the prosecutor once more would give her strength. Tears burned her eyes.

"I'm not asking you to go."

"I know. Please don't ask me not to."

She nodded, and he stooped to kiss her cheek before he left.

Dan dialed Jim Hight's number during his break. Hight's secretary put him through, and the lawyer said wearily in his ear, "I know, I know, Ryan. I heard early this morning. I was about to call Laurel."

"Her probation officer told her. What has the prosecution got?"

"It seems Lieutenant Dryer hasn't been as slack as we supposed. He came up with a few factors that may influence the outcome of the trial. The judge decided it was enough and set an early date."

"What did Dryer come up with?"

"Well, there was some irregularity about Mr. Hatcher's car."

"The Corvette? I knew it!" Dan felt almost exultant.

"Laurel tried to claim it after Bob died. We filed a civil suit, trying to get her personal belongings back and get a settlement on the house and contents. Wayne and Renata

Hatcher are trying to use that to show Laurel was tired of the marriage and killed him for his money."

"That's old." Dan ran a hand through his hair.

"I know, but this civil suit is becoming an issue in the criminal case. If she truly loved him, why fight his parents over the house they paid for?"

"For crying out loud, it was a gift! A wedding gift."

"Take it easy," Hight said. "I'm on your side. We're pushing for a fat settlement. Laurel was wronged in this. Her mother-in-law just waltzed in and claimed everything while Laurel was in jail. Furniture, art, everything. That all should have gone to Laurel. The Corvette may be another story."

"Why? It belonged to her husband."

"Yes, but it was in Bob's name only, not Laurel's. Jack Brody now claims it was a business perk, and Hatcher & Brody should have the car back."

"Oh, slick," said Dan.

"Something else came up. It's unrelated to the murder trial, but it may bear on it indirectly. It concerns the project Bob Hatcher was working on when he died—the Maple Grove bridge in New Hampshire."

"What about it?"

"I'll fax you what they gave me. There's some question now over whether the materials were up to spec. The state is performing an on-site inspection and has subpoenaed some documents relating to the contract. I'm meeting with Dryer and the district attorney this afternoon. Perhaps I'll have more news after that."

"All right, but make sure you send me everything, Hight. Every shred."

"At Mrs. Hatcher's request?"

"Naturally."

"How did she take the news?" Hight asked.

"She's a bit shaken up by it. I'm coming with her to Maine."

"Thought you might. When will you arrive?" Hight sounded more affable than before.

"As soon as possible. We'll let you know."

"All right. I'll put my investigator on these new concerns right away, but I could use another man."

"I've got the private investigator's license," Dan said. "It came through today."

"Well, that's a start." Hight's voice held a new optimism. "It's not a Maine license, but I might be able to get permission to use you temporarily, on this one case. Especially since you're coming with Mrs. Hatcher. If she officially hired you in Ohio…yes, I think that would work."

Dan hung up feeling that at last things were moving. Something was going to happen, for better or worse, and he would stand by Laurel until it was finished. Then they both could decide whether they could have a future together. He took a deep breath and headed for his lieutenant's desk.

"It's only an extra week," he told Lieutenant Powers. "Three of vacation, one of leave without pay. Two weeks to poke around before the trial, two weeks to wrap it up."

"What if the trial drags on?" Powers asked.

"It won't. Will it?"

"You never know." The lieutenant frowned at him. "There's been some talk about this."

"Seems everybody knows about Laurel," Dan agreed.

Jessica had come to him about the gossip in the duty room, and he knew there was no stopping it.

"I'm sorry," Powers said. "I tried to maintain confidentiality, but when you came in the other night to report being shot at, and then your name turned up on the P.I.'s list, I had to explain the background to the patrol sergeant."

Dan nodded. "It's all right. I didn't exactly hide what I was doing."

Powers pulled off his glasses and rubbed his eyelids. "I don't like this business, Ryan. You'll get to Maine and not want to come back."

"Oh, come on, I've never done anything like that before."

"You've never been in love before, at least not when I was your supervisor."

Dan smiled. It was probably a lopsided, silly smile. He couldn't help it. Things were happening at the speed of light, but nothing could keep him from Laurel's side as she faced her ordeal.

"You know I'm going, no matter what."

"Yes, I know that. I think the best thing would be to give you a leave of absence." Powers rummaged in his desk drawer and extracted a form, then consulted his calendar. "Let's see… Twelve weeks ought to do it, don't you think?"

Dan stared at him. "Three months? Just like that?"

"Can you afford it?"

"I'll manage but…if things are settled before then, can I come back early?"

"Absolutely. You can have your vacation pay in advance." Powers signed his name with a flourish. "I'll send that upstairs right away. Do me a favor, Ryan. Get this out of your system. Come back ready to work."

Once again Laurel went through the unpacking routine. It seemed pointless to hang her clothes in the closet. But this time there was a difference. She was hanging them in Dan's closet.

She arranged her few dresses and blouses carefully. She could hear Dan in the living room, moving things around so he could set up her computer. His police uniforms hung next to her clothes, and she touched the nearest shirt gingerly. She knew Dan loved his job, but he was leaving it for her.

"I think you're all set," he said from the doorway, and she shut the closet door and turned to face him.

"Thanks. You didn't have to connect the computer."

He shrugged. "It will give you something to do while I finish out the workweek."

"Do you think…" She hesitated, not wanting to ask the same questions over and over.

"Judy will be here in an hour. Jessica's bringing her in an unmarked car."

She nodded. "Good. I don't want anyone seeing her car. Not now."

Dan stepped toward her. "It's going to be okay. I'll stay at Judy's in case anyone tries to break in there again."

Laurel knew it was a real possibility. The house swap had seemed logical when Dan suggested it. She and Judy would stay together at his little rental, and Dan would sleep at Judy's home until Friday, when his vacation period would start. Then the two of them would head for Maine, and Judy's sister would arrive to stay with her. Judy could move back into her house with some assurance of safety, since the garage door had been repaired and she had contracted for a security system. Jessica had promised to keep an eye on her, just to be sure.

"Anything else I can do?" Dan asked.

"I don't think so." Laurel took the few remaining items from her duffel bag. She set her cosmetic bag on the dresser and looked down at the framed photograph in her hand.

"Is that Bob?"

"Both of us."

"May I?" he asked reverently.

She held the frame out, watching Dan's face. He studied the picture for a long moment.

"You look happy."

She swallowed hard. "We were." She leaned closer and stared at herself in the photograph. She looked young. Carefree.

"You're more beautiful now," Dan said softly. He reached out to stroke her hair, and she closed her eyes, enjoying his touch for a second. If she leaned toward him, he would fold her in his arms. She smiled at him and stepped away. It would be too easy to try to make things happen her own way and not wait for God's leading.

Dan set the frame on the dresser. "You need to hire me as your private investigator. Hight's orders."

"All right. What's your fee?"

"A penny a year."

They both laughed.

"What did he tell you about his meeting with the D.A.?" she asked.

"The state is looking at the bridge project Bob was last overseeing."

"The Maple Grove bridge?"

"Yes. Something about the materials. Hight faxed me some documents at the police station, but I haven't had time to look at them yet." He stepped toward her once more and raised her chin so that she looked into his eyes. "I would never let you go back alone."

She caught his hand and squeezed it, then moved back, fighting tears. "How can you do this?"

"I told you, vacation. I've been saving it. Didn't know what for."

She nodded, not trusting herself to continue this line of conversation. "We'd better get you something to eat."

"Sounds good. I picked up a few groceries." He took her into the kitchen and opened the refrigerator. "I guess there's no one you can stay with in Maine?"

She shook her head. "I can't think of anyone."

"The state doesn't pay to put up defendants, eh?"

"Not unless they house them at the jail."

"Well, we'll work something out." She wondered if he'd gone through the same mental exercise she had, counting his savings and ticking off his credit card limits. It would be expensive to put two of them up in a hotel for several weeks. Maybe Jim Hight would have some ideas.

Dan arranged a packaged steak and an assortment of salad vegetables on the counter. "Think you can sleep in another strange bed tonight?"

"I'll be all right once Judy's here."

"Good. Just don't lie awake thinking about the case."

"But I need to think about it, Dan. I even took that

picture out of the frame to see if there was anything behind it, but there wasn't." She frowned in frustration. "They think there's something significant, you said."

"Seems that way."

"Then it has to be something I had before I went to jail. Something Bob had access to." She shook her head, wishing she could clear her mind of all the extraneous details and home in on what was important. "I went through all my things again, but nothing jumped out at me."

She began making a salad while Dan placed a frying pan on the stove. He turned toward her. "So tell me whatever you know about this bridge project."

Judy again volunteered to go through records with them. She curled up in an armchair, eagerly accepting the papers Dan gave her.

"You don't have to spend your evening doing this," Laurel said.

"It's fun. Well, maybe not fun exactly, but it's stimulating…and I'm glad to be back with you two."

"I missed you terribly. I'm glad your sister's coming."

"Thanks. My boss arranged a low-profile rental car for me for the rest of this week, and I'm taking some vacation time soon. My sister and I may take a trip together, to get away for a while."

Laurel wished she could get away—away from her life. But that was impossible, so she took a report and skimmed it. "These are the specifications for the Maple Grove bridge."

"Mean anything to you?" Dan asked.

"Not really. I know Bob was stressed over the project."

"Why?"

She considered. "I think they'd cut it close on their bid."

"Well, I told you a question's arisen as to whether or not they actually used the specified materials."

Judy laid down her sheaf of papers. "Why would this bridge thing make them send Laurel back to trial?"

"It wouldn't, by itself."

"There's something else?"

"Well, yes." Dan glanced at Laurel.

"They found new evidence against me?"

Dan hesitated. "They're making a fuss about the civil suit." He turned to Judy. "Laurel's in-laws took just about everything she owned while Laurel was in jail."

"She told me. I don't see how they got away with it."

Laurel shrugged. "Me, either. Renata said she took back the things they had paid for." It had baffled Laurel at the time, but she'd accepted it along with all the other injustices.

"She's a thief," said Judy.

"I wasn't in a position to make a stink about it." Laurel toyed with the edge of the couch cushion.

"Those things were yours," Dan said. "The house and furnishings should have been part of the estate."

"My lawyer filed a motion of some sort, but a lot of things had already been sold, and apparently Wayne and Renata came up with receipts that showed they'd paid for it all. I never got a cent."

"I can't believe it," Judy said in dismay.

"I walked out with my clothes, a few boxes of books and mementos and my wedding ring. That was it." Laurel sighed.

"Maybe if I'd been less distraught, I could have put up a better fight."

"Well, Jim Hight is still fighting for you," Dan assured her. "He told me last night that the civil suit will come up soon, and he still hopes to reach a cash settlement in your favor, even if you can't get the things back."

Laurel nodded. "The things themselves didn't mean that much. I'd have gladly given up the house and furniture to have Bob alive."

Dan squeezed her hand.

Judy stood up. "Let's have dessert." She stopped in the kitchen doorway and looked back at Laurel. "You have the right to feel that way, honey, but I hope Bob Hatcher was the man you think he was."

When they were alone, Dan chose his words carefully.

"Laurel, I've got to tell you, the Hatchers are saying this civil suit proves you cared more about Bob's things than you did about him." Her stricken look got to him, and he said hastily, "Jim knows that's crazy. He figures it will backfire, and show how hateful they were to you."

Laurel shuddered. "It's just like Renata. She wants to see me imprisoned for life."

She was still frightened. Dan didn't blame her—it scared him, too. His bravado was tested when he considered what the Hatchers and the criminal justice system had already done to Laurel. "Well, we hope things will go better this time, right?"

She managed a smile.

Judy came back with a tray of cookies and lemonade. "Do you know yet when you're leaving for Maine?"

"Saturday," Dan said. "That is, if Laurel's willing. I got a leave of absence. Three weeks before the trial, twelve weeks total."

"Twelve weeks? Dan, really?" Laurel asked.

"Yes. If I don't need it all, I'll come back early."

Laurel's lip trembled. "Thank you."

They discussed the case for a few minutes longer while they ate the cookies, then Dan looked at his watch. "I'd better get going. I told my folks I'd drive out there tonight."

"I thought you were staying at my place," Judy said.

"I am, but I need to let them know what's going on."

Dan drew Laurel into the entry, where his suitcase waited.

"We'll get through this with God's help," he whispered, placing his hands on her shoulders.

Her eyes were luminous. "I want to believe that."

The moment seemed perfect, so he bent down and brushed her lips with his. It jolted him to the core and he drew her closer when she slipped her hands around him. He realized he was prolonging the embrace beyond his intention, but he couldn't help lingering.

When she pulled away, he held on to her. His heart would break if they lost the trial.

"Laurel, when it's over—"

She caught her breath. "Danny, I can't talk about that yet. You know I can't."

She was right, of course, and now was not the time to let his feelings run wild. She needed his professional skills, and he needed to remember to be cautious.

She pushed gently away from him. "I can't have you thinking things are settled when they're not. It wouldn't be fair to anyone."

He took a deep breath. "You're right. You're innocent, Laurel. I believe God will honor that."

She pressed her lips together and looked away. "I hope so, but I could be in jail for more than twenty years."

"If that happens, I'll be here for you."

Her eyes narrowed. "Don't be foolish. If it does happen, you need to go on with your life."

"Laurel—"

"Please don't say any more. Not now. I knew this would be too hard." She turned and walked quickly from the room.

Dan felt like kicking himself. He'd been stupid to let his emotions spiral out of control like that when she was agonizing over this thing. He needed to be strong for her. Levelheaded. Logical. He left quietly, locking the door behind him.

ELEVEN

Dan faced off with his parents across the kitchen table. "Dad, Mom, you have to realize that Laurel is innocent."

"Of course she is," his mother retorted. "My son wouldn't devote his life to a dangerous, conniving woman."

Dan smiled. His mother's heart was boundless. He'd seen it when his brother Owen chose his bride. Marissa was as dear to her as her own children now.

"A hung jury, son." Caution edged his father's voice. "That's not so good."

"That's why we've been working so hard to uncover something new that will help her."

"Find anything yet?" His father's large hands closed around his coffee mug.

"I can outline the case for you," Dan offered.

Michael nodded. He was a cabinetmaker, and he knew the value of detail work.

"Well, you can excuse me," Kathryn said. "I'll be making pies. You are bringing that poor little thing to meet us and have supper, aren't you, Daniel?"

"I'm afraid not, Mom. You'll have to wait a few weeks to meet Laurel. We'll be heading for Maine Saturday."

"Already?"

"Yes. Her lawyer thinks I can help him with the investigation between now and the trial. I'll let you know where we're staying."

"You tell her we're behind her, you understand?"

Dan smiled. "Of course, Mom. Should I tell Becky and the boys?"

"We'll fill them in if you want," Michael said. "There won't be any embarrassing moments for her in this house."

"Thank you." Relief surged over Dan. He ought to have come home sooner and told them. Owen's willingness to help had been an indication of how the rest of the family would feel. The people he trusted most would share the load, and he couldn't ask for anything more than that.

"Come on." His father rose with his mug in his hand. "I'll show you what I'm working on."

Dan followed him out the back door, into his workshop. His father had remodeled the old carriage house. The place smelled of cedar shavings and pine, with a whiff of turpentine. Dan loved the shop where his father crafted beautiful furniture.

"This is a special order," Michael said, running his hand over the smooth top of a dry sink. "Just need to put the hardware on."

Dan always wondered at his father's humility. He took pride in his superior work, but was self-effacing as an artist. He'd always taught the boys to do their best and give God the glory for any talent they had.

"This girl, son." Michael turned toward him, his eyes as somber as Dan's. "What will you do if things don't go her way in the courtroom?"

Dan took a deep breath. "She won't promise me anything until the trial is over."

Michael nodded. "That's as it should be."

"Yes. But I love her, Dad."

"Have you told her that?"

"Not in so many words. She…thinks we should go slow until the verdict is in."

Michael's features softened. "She's right, you know, Danny."

Dan nodded, though his heart was torn. "I want to do things right, Dad. But she's innocent. I'm going to support her through this."

His father studied him intently. "And if she's found guilty?"

Dan sighed and picked up a chisel, examining the keen edge. "She'll still be innocent."

"Ah, boy, you always were stubborn."

"What's the difference between stubborn and loyal?" Dan asked.

"I recall that girl you were going around with a while ago. Ashleigh."

"This isn't like that, Dad." Dan inhaled deeply and started over. "Ashleigh needed a different kind of help. She needed Christ, but she wouldn't accept that. Laurel is a believer. Her faith is true, even though she's been through an ordeal worse than we can imagine. She told me…she told me God will be with her, no matter how this turns out. And I want to be there, too."

"We'll pray about this, your mother and I." His father clasped his shoulder with a strong hand. "And Laurel is right. God will uphold you, son. Through the good and the bad."

* * *

On Tuesday, Judy went to work and Laurel cleaned the sparsely furnished house and rested. Time and again her mind went back to Dan. His face had become so dear, his earnest endeavor to help her precious. She yearned to believe as he did that they could have a future together. A rambling old white house with lilac bushes in front and a vegetable garden behind. A porch swing, a dog…and children. Dan's love and protection.

But the bars of the county jail superimposed themselves over the daydreams. She would not let him lock himself into a promise with that in view. She kept busy, but still the thoughts came.

"What smells so good?" Judy asked when she came home.

"Banana bread. It was bake and scrub the bathroom, or go crazy thinking about the case."

Judy set a bag of groceries on the counter. "Great. Did you get the bathroom cleaned yet?"

"It sparkles."

"I knew you were the perfect roommate the moment I saw you."

Laurel grinned. "I wish I could stay longer with you, but that's not to be. We're taking a chance staying here together as it is."

"I was extra careful driving home," Judy admitted. "I'm sure no one followed me."

"I'm so sorry!"

"Let's not start that again. Just remember that I'm keeping your room open at the house for when you come back."

"That's sweet."

"Where are you and Dan staying in Maine?"

"A hotel, I suppose." Laurel walked out to the garage with Judy for more groceries. "It could be an expensive trip for Dan, just to see me convicted." She reached into the back of the car for a sack.

Judy laid a hand on her arm. "Stop that! You are not going to be convicted. It would infuriate Dan to hear you say that."

"I'll try to be more positive," Laurel said tentatively.

"Well, that's more like it." Judy grabbed the last bag of food. "Look, I know this trial is about you, but you must realize what it's doing to Dan."

"What do you mean?"

"He's putting everything on the line for you."

Laurel slowly trailed her to the kitchen. "I can see all that he's doing for me."

Judy faced her, a plaintive look on her face. "He loves you, you know."

Laurel set her bag on the table. "I…can't consider that right now. When I know the verdict, then I can think about love and the future and having a life. If it's a good verdict."

Judy shook her head. "You can't talk that way to Dan. Don't let him feel like he has to hold you up, too. He wants to go out and slay dragons for you. He'll have a lot better chance if you quit tripping him up with negative thinking."

Laurel sat down at the table. "You think it would make that big a difference?"

"Of course." Judy leaned down and wagged a finger under Laurel's nose. "It's awfully hard for knights in shining armor to get up again once they fall."

* * *

Dan arrived before supper, wearing his uniform.

"I wasn't sure you'd come tonight," Laurel said.

"What, because of last night?"

She nodded. "I was pretty rough on you."

"No, you were practical. I need that sometimes."

She smiled warily. "At least I know how you feel now."

"You know some of it," he agreed. "I'll tell you the rest sometime. When you're ready."

She bit her bottom lip. "I think I'd like to hear it…when the time is right."

He resisted the urge to pull her into his arms. They went to the kitchen, where Judy was setting the table.

"Have you bought your plane tickets yet?" Judy asked.

"I thought we'd drive," Dan said.

Judy nodded. "Slower, but cheaper." She took a meat loaf from the oven and set it on the hot mat. "I've decided to take a couple of weeks' vacation while you're in Maine."

"Good," said Laurel. "You need a break from all the headaches we've given you."

Judy and Dan sat down while Laurel speared the baked potatoes with a fork and plopped them into a serving dish.

Judy said, "Actually, I might see you during my vacation."

Laurel froze. "You're…going to the trial?"

"Not necessarily. But my sister, Jackie, can't get away as soon as I'd like to go, and I found myself envying you two and your trip to Maine. So I went online and found the classified ads from the *Kennebec Journal*. I'm renting a cottage on a lake for a few weeks. Jackie will join me when she's able." She smiled at them.

Dan eyed her suspiciously. "Judy, you're being sneaky. What's up?"

"Nothing. It's just that I found I could rent this three-bedroom cottage for half the price of a good hotel room. It's stocked with linens and dishes, has a dock and a rowboat. I thought, 'Why not? I'll just soak up the sun in Maine for a couple of weeks.'" She turned eagerly to Laurel, then back to Dan. "How about it?"

"It's brilliant," Dan said. "Wish I'd thought of it."

"Dan booked rooms for us in Augusta," Laurel said.

"Great." Judy unfolded her napkin. "For the first week. But I hope you'll consider spending weeks two and three with me on the lake. It's fifteen miles from the courthouse. I checked."

"You're asking us to stay with you?" Dan looked eagerly at Laurel. Even though Laurel instinctively hated the idea of her friend seeing her on trial, he knew Judy's presence would bring her comfort.

"It would save you a bundle, and I don't like to vacation alone." Judy sounded determined.

"We'll pay half," Dan said firmly.

Judy shrugged. "If you insist, but it's really unnecessary."

She scooped a generous portion of meat loaf onto her plate. "I'll run errands and cook. Anything to help you out. And if you want me to stay away from the courthouse when the time comes, I will."

Laurel pushed her chair back and opened her arms to Judy. "You are the dearest friend I've ever had. How can you do this?"

"Hey, I hate vacationing alone."

* * *

Judy insisted on doing the dishes after supper, and Dan and Laurel settled in the living room with the briefcase.

"What did you learn from compiling all this information?" Laurel stared at the folders of documents.

Dan took both her hands in his. "Mostly, I learned you really loved this guy."

She nodded, and tears welled in her eyes. "He wasn't perfect, but he was decent."

"The two of you talked about him leaving Hatcher & Brody as late as March that year," Dan noted.

"Yes. He wanted to be independent of the family, but his dad begged him to stay. And Uncle Jack had given him that car. I thought it was an attempt to make him feel guilty, you know? So he wouldn't leave them."

"But why did they care so much? Was it a matter of pride for Wayne Hatcher to have his son in the firm? Or was it just anger that he would consider leaving?"

"Maybe a little of both." The ache of Bob's disharmony with his family came back to her. He had wanted his parents to have the faith he had and to love Laurel as a daughter. But his intercession for her had only seemed to alienate Renata further, and both parents refused to listen to him about spiritual matters.

She faced Dan with new resolution, eager to go on and learn the truth about Bob's death. "Bob wanted to please his folks with his work, and he wanted them to love me. He tried several times to talk to Renata about the way she treated me, but that only seemed to make her angrier."

"Near the end," Dan said, "you told me Bob was stressed, and you thought he wasn't telling you everything."

"I was frightened," she admitted. "When the Maple Grove bridge came up, Bob was upset for weeks. I'm not positive the bids had anything to do with it, but that was all I could figure. I asked him about it twice, but he didn't want to talk about it. The second time, he said, 'Laurel, just let it be. When I can tell you about it, I will.'"

"But he never did."

"No. I never knew how they did it, but they always underbid their competitors, just enough to get the contract and still make a good profit. Simon Brothers accused Wayne of cheating somehow. Wayne denied it, and the next time, when they were bidding on the airport in Lewiston, Hatcher & Brody bid too high. But Bob told me afterward that his father didn't want that project, anyway."

"So Bob thought Wayne bid high on it just to mollify the competitors?" Dan asked.

She nodded. "He told me that much. When the bridge project came up, he wouldn't talk about it. But he was trusting the Lord, even then. I know he was. He read his Bible a lot, and we would pray together. I guess he thought I was better off not knowing the details."

"Hatcher & Brody was the lowest bidder on the bridge," Dan said.

"Not actually, but they promised to use this special kind of steel—oh!" She clapped her hand to her mouth.

"What is it?"

"You said the prosecutor mentioned inferior materials being used in the bridge."

Dan nodded. "The city of Maple Grove filed a complaint. The flanges on some of the beams had cracked. It scared them, so the state of New Hampshire sent out an inspector.

He claims the girders were made from a lower grade of steel than the plans called for. Hatcher & Brody is having to spend a lot of money to repair it."

"I can't believe they would do that," Laurel said. "How could they? It would ruin their reputation."

Dan shrugged. "I'm just telling you what the report says."

Laurel didn't like where her thoughts were heading. "But substandard materials? I mean, they're not stupid. People could be killed."

Dan reached for the briefcase. "Let me take that spec list and compare it with the inspector's report."

"Do you think maybe Bob knew they'd substituted the materials and made a fuss about it?"

"As a motive, you mean?"

She nodded. "The bridge wasn't actually finished until the fall after Bob's death. We have the report of the engineer who took over the project, don't we?"

"Yes, they completed it five months later, just under the bid."

"So, maybe they underbid their competitors, then realized they couldn't do it for that amount."

Dan frowned. "If they decided to cut corners instead of taking the loss, and Bob got wind of it—"

"Of course," said Laurel. "He was the project manager. He was right out there when the materials were delivered. If something shady was going on in that project, he'd have known."

"When did Hatcher & Brody start laying in the materials?"

"Over the winter. Bob made several trips to Maple

Grove to keep an eye on things. I went down a couple of times and stayed through the week at the motel with him." She paused. "But if someone was substituting low-grade materials, they could have brought in the cheaper stuff anytime Bob wasn't there."

"Yes," Dan reflected. "That would upset Bob when he discovered it."

"But this is all speculation. It could have been someone else in the company, not his family."

"When did Uncle Jack give him the car?"

She glanced at him uneasily. "January, I think."

"Before his first trip to Maple Grove?"

"Yes. He drove it down there the first time." She stared at Dan as she thought about that. "You're saying the Corvette is somehow related to the bridge project. Jack wanted Bob to keep quiet about the shoddy materials, so he gave him the car in advance."

"If he'd given it to him after Bob saw the switch, it would have been a little obvious," Dan said. "This way, it just made him feel guilty to have to do something that would hurt his nice old Uncle Jack."

"Bob would have reported it to Wayne," Laurel insisted.

"And if Wayne already knew about it?"

Laurel tried to get a deep breath, but she felt as if her lungs were constricted. "Bob just wouldn't let that happen."

Dan laid the papers on the coffee table and slid closer. "I don't want to upset you, but we've got to consider the possibility that Bob knew about it."

She jumped to her feet. "All right, maybe he did. But if he had suspicions, he'd look for proof as to who was responsible. And if he had proof, he wouldn't look the other way and take bribes. He'd confront that person." She shouted the words, unable to hold back the panic that filled her.

"I think he did," Dan said gently. "On May twenty-eighth. At your house, while you were shopping in Bangor."

Laurel stared at him, then turned and walked slowly toward her bedroom. When the door closed, Dan joined Judy in the kitchen and told her of his confrontation with Laurel. "She can't accept the idea that he knew and didn't call the police."

"Maybe Bob was trying to get solid proof before he reported it," Judy said thoughtfully.

"I think he had proof," Dan said. "That's what those thugs were after when they attacked us. Bob had something that would implicate the killer, and they believe Laurel has it now."

"Why didn't it come out before, when she went to trial last winter?"

"I don't know." Dan sighed. "What do I do now?"

"Just wait. Give her time to absorb this. Then ask her if she's ready for you to discuss this theory with the lawyer."

Judy made a pot of coffee and brought him a mug in the living room. Dan sat on the couch, staring at the bouquet of daffodils Judy had placed on the coffee table that evening. It made a bright splash in the room of neutral colors, the way Laurel had splashed into his ordinary life.

Judy sat down on the arm of the sofa. "She's been through so much, Dan."

He nodded, his lips tight together. "I've tried not to think about it too much, but I know it was terrible."

"Discovering the body in itself was traumatic," Judy agreed. "What came after would have put most people over the edge."

He glanced toward the closed bedroom door. "Maybe I should stop talking about it. Just leave her be. But I can't help thinking there's more to this."

"Those men who shot at you were certain."

Dan sensed her anger and squeezed her arm. "I'd say I'm sorry again, but after the first hundred times it loses its impact."

Judy smiled ruefully. "Don't make the same mistake again, Dan."

"You mean, don't park Laurel here at my house too long?"

"They found her before."

"Yes. But I can't leave until Friday. My superiors are being generous as it is."

She sipped her coffee. "I can take her to a hotel the last couple of nights, if you think it would be safer."

That was like Judy, worrying about anyone but herself. "We'll see. Thanks."

The bedroom door creaked open, and Laurel came out. Her face was streaked with tears and her eyes red-rimmed.

"Excuse me," Judy murmured, and she disappeared into the kitchen with the empty mugs.

Dan stood and waited for Laurel to speak. She stopped three feet from him and met his eyes.

"If it happened that way," she whispered, "why didn't he tell me?"

Dan took one step and held her in his arms. He cradled her head against his shoulder, caressing her hair, thankful that she had come back to him for comfort.

"I think he wanted to protect you. If you didn't know, no one could accuse you of spilling the beans. He was going to expose them, sweetheart. That's why they had to stop him."

Her hands fluttered against his chest, and she shook her head. "His parents couldn't do that, could they? Kill their own child in cold blood?"

"Maybe not, but what about Jack Brody? Maybe he was behind all of it—the underbidding, the poor materials, everything—and Bob knew. Bribes didn't work. Bob was going to turn him in. Does that make sense?"

"I don't know. We have no proof Jack is the killer."

"They have no proof it was you, either. If we can cast enough suspicion on Jack, the jury will have doubts about you."

"Is that a successful type of defense, Dan? I want to be found innocent. I don't just want to be not guilty because of reasonable doubt."

He wanted that, too. He wanted the world to acknowledge her innocence. He wanted to see it in print—that Bob Hatcher was killed because he was an honest man, not because his greedy wife wanted his money and her freedom.

He ran his hands over her tense shoulders and her rigid back.

"We're going to find out the truth, and when we do, everybody will know it. They'll know you didn't do it, and they'll know Bob was a hero. He was a good man in a bad situation, and he tried to fix it. We won't forget that he stood up to them. We won't ever forget."

Laurel leaned limply against him. "Danny, he's in heaven."

"I know, sweetheart. And I'm glad."

"You would have liked him," she whispered.

"I think so."

TWELVE

Dan puttered around in the kitchen of his house Thursday evening while Judy helped Laurel with her packing. Although Laurel had few possessions, she seemed to find the task overwhelming. When he ventured to the bedroom doorway, she was looking uncertainly around the room where she had slept for the past three nights.

"Maybe I should just take all my things."

"You're coming back," Judy said firmly.

Dan leaned with one arm on the door frame. "Leave the computer for sure, and anything else you don't think you'll need on the trip."

Laurel sighed. "I wish I knew how many clothes to take, and what Jim will want me to wear to court."

"Just use your best judgment," Judy said softly.

"I'd better take my black skirt. Jim told me to go with widow's weeds the first time around, but that wasn't too successful. Maybe he'll want sophisticated this time, or professional, or an ingenue look, although I'm a bit old for that. Girl next door, perhaps. Should I take this?" Laurel held out a yellow gingham jumper.

"That's cute on you," Judy said.

Dan said nothing, but his heart ached.

"Maybe frilly feminine is good," Laurel choked. "But I'll have to shop up there in that case. Oh, what am I doing? It's not going to matter." She burst into sobs, and Judy hurried to embrace her.

"Honey, honey, it's okay."

Choked up himself and sensing the two women needed some privacy, Dan went back to the kitchen and leaned on the smooth countertop. He hated how helpless he felt for not being able to alleviate Laurel's suffering. He'd tried to handle all the details of the trip for her, and everything had come together: the leave of absence, the private investigator's license, the reservations, the timing. He had five hundred dollars in his pocket, a gift from his father. He'd hung his uniforms away in the closet, packing only his civilian clothes.

Until now it had almost seemed he and Laurel were planning an enjoyable outing together. But the reality of her uncertain future and the stress it caused her could no longer be ignored.

Judy came in from the next room, and he tried to smile, but it slipped into a grimace.

"Is she okay?" he asked.

"She needs a good night's sleep. Why don't you go finish your arrangements and come back tomorrow."

"We could leave when I get off work tomorrow if she wants to."

"No, let Laurel sleep here and start out early Saturday. You'll both be rested, and you'll have a whole day ahead of you to drive. Less complicated that way."

He nodded. "I've got a few things to take care of."

"Did you pack your violin?" Judy asked.

He smiled. "Yes, but do you think that's a good idea? I won't have time to practice."

"You'd better. I want us to do that Haydn piece this fall."

"Yes, Mother."

Judy patted his cheek. "I'll see you tomorrow night. Plan to have supper with us."

Dan got out of his truck at the police station on Friday. The late May morning promised warmth and clear skies. He whistled the first few notes of the Beethoven they'd played in the concert, but squinted as he turned. A man sat on a bench in the little park across the street. A civilian, peering at Dan over the top of his newspaper. Probably nothing. Even so, before joining Jessica in the duty room, he called Laurel to warn her to stay in the house and keep the drapes drawn.

He and Jessica were called to the scene of a minor automobile accident that afternoon. The driver Dan questioned was too inebriated to give coherent answers, and Dan put him in the back of the squad car.

As Dan shut the door, his cell phone trilled. He ignored it, but grew more anxious as it continued. He walked to the front of the car and checked it. Judy. He'd only given her the number after the thugs had threatened him and Laurel at her house Saturday night.

"Judy, what's up?"

"I'm so sorry to call you at work, Dan."

"No problem. What's happened?"

"A man came to my office asking about Laurel. Dan, you've got to move her tonight. He threatened me."

"Are you okay?"

"Yes, and I called security. That's why he left."

"Good. Make a police report." Dan leaned back against the hood of the squad car. "What did he look like?"

"Five-ten, two hundred and twenty pounds, Caucasian, dark hair and eyes," Judy said.

"You're good. Call Laurel and tell her to have her things ready. I'll pick her up as soon as I can. No, wait. Send a cab around for her."

"To take her where?"

Dan sighed. "We need to get her to a safe location right away."

"Marcia Smith's house? It's out of town."

Jessica put her hands on her hips and glared at him. He could tell she was annoyed at the interruption.

Dan straightened and headed for the passenger door of the squad car. "Sure, if you can set it up. Make sure you're not being tailed by anyone suspicious. I'll pick Laurel up there, but I may not be able to get away until after five."

He shoved his phone into his pocket and got in the car.

"Personal life interfering with the job?" Jessica murmured, eyeing him anxiously as she stowed her gear.

"Just a bit. I'm sorry."

"If you really need to leave, I can handle this," she said.

"It's okay."

She shook her head. "I told you, you should have let the P.D. protect Laurel."

"Let's just finish up here, okay?"

Jessica frowned. "She wouldn't have called you if it wasn't important. What do you need?"

"Nothing. Just…can we dump this guy at the station and drive by my house?"

"I'll book him. You take a run over there."

"Thanks, Jess."

"I'm going to miss you while you're away. Send me a postcard."

At four-thirty, Dan pulled his pickup into Marcia's long gravel driveway. The llamas in the pasture crowded the fence to look at him.

Marcia met him at the door, smiling. "I like your girl, Dan."

"Thanks." He bent to kiss Marcia's cheek. "Sorry to drag you into this."

She brushed that aside and took him to the living room where Laurel waited. He was surprised to find Judy there, as well.

Laurel jumped up and hurried to him.

"All set?" Dan asked.

"Yes, if you are."

"My things are in the truck." He nodded at Judy. "You all right?"

"I'm fine. I hope you don't mind my coming to see you off. I took a cab and was extremely careful that I wasn't being followed."

He smiled, hoping his friends hadn't drawn Laurel's stalkers once more. "You kept your wits and put the police on that fellow. I wouldn't be surprised if they've got him already." It was a bit of a stretch—he'd checked before leaving the police station, and the man who had accosted Judy was still at liberty. But that had influenced Jessica to urge him to leave early.

"We're going to miss you and Judy something fierce,"

Marcia said. "The quartet is going to go to pot this summer, with both our violinists taking extended vacations."

Dan smiled. "You and Joe can get together and practice. You'll be way ahead of us when we come back."

"Well, I hope the police catch that fellow." Marcia shook her head at the audacity of it. "Coming to your office to bother you, Judy."

"If any strangers show up here, you call the cops immediately," Judy warned her.

Dan picked up Laurel's bag, and Judy went out with them to the truck. Marcia stood in the doorway watching them.

"Should we meet you somewhere when you come to Maine?" Dan asked Judy.

"No, I'm flying to Portland and renting a car. I'll call your cell phone when I get to the lake."

Laurel clung to Judy for a moment. "I'm sorry I was such a crybaby last night."

"Shh, forget it. Take care of Dan. And remember, for the next few days, you'll be the only one there to polish his armor."

Laurel smiled and kissed her cheek, then slid into the truck.

Judy went to Dan, and he threw his arms around her in a huge hug.

"You've done so much. Thank you," he said.

"She's all yours now. I'll pray for the best."

As they drove away from Marcia's house, Laurel felt the cloud of fear lift. She determined not to brood the whole way and focused on happier topics.

"Tell me more about your family." She settled her purse

and sweater on the seat between them. "I want to hear it all. Little League, first puppy, sibling rivalry. I expect to know everything about you by the time we reach Maine." She touched his arm, and Dan smiled at her. "Tell me all the details. What did your first lunch box look like?"

He laughed. "Sorry, I was a hot-lunch man."

"Oh. What was your favorite meal at the cafeteria?"

Dan pulled out onto a state highway and looked in the rearview mirror. His face tensed, and he floored the gas pedal. "Hang on."

She looked out the rear window and saw a low blue car momentarily drop behind them, then put on speed to overtake them.

Amazing how quickly the fear returned.

He approached a crossroad swiftly, then braked and tore around the corner with the truck on two wheels.

Laurel gasped and held on to the gun rack in the back window, watching behind them. The blue car followed at a slightly more prudent speed.

"Cell phone."

Dan's words were clipped, and she could read the tension in his face.

"Where?"

"Shirt pocket."

She pulled it out, then looked at him. "Who am I calling?"

"Nine-one-one."

She gulped, dialed, and handed him the phone. He slowed down a little and took it. The blue car closed the distance between them.

"I'm on the county road, and there's a vehicle pursuing me. Can you send an officer out here ASAP?"

The blue car came on fast.

"Danny! He's going to hit us!"

Too late, Dan floored the gas. The impact made the pickup bounce and swerve, but Dan regained control. He threw the cell phone toward her, but Laurel was unable to catch it and it fell to the floor.

"Hold on!" he yelled.

The car crept up beside him, and Dan began to brake.

"Is he passing us?" Laurel pulled her seat belt tighter.

"She. And don't bet on it."

The car's impact came on Dan's door and the front fender, throwing the light truck toward the shoulder and triggering Dan's side air bag. They veered off the pavement, and Dan clung to the wheel, his face set like granite as he struggled to keep control.

Laurel closed her eyes and braced herself. The truck bounced and lunged, then came to rest. Slowly she opened her eyes. They sat on the edge of a hay field, facing the road. The blue car was parked on the shoulder just beyond, and walking rapidly toward them was a slender, dark-haired woman in a red silk blouse and jeans.

Dan watched in amazement as Laurel unfastened her seat belt with trembling fingers and leaped from the truck, her face livid.

"I always knew you were crazy, but this beats all! You idiot!"

"Who you calling crazy?" the woman demanded. "I'm smart enough to find you, and smart enough to know who my friends are."

"*Friends?*" Laurel shrieked. "Oh, pardon me. Haven't you heard? Friends don't assassinate friends."

Against his better judgment, Dan stepped between them. "Ladies, ladies."

Laurel shouted, "She almost killed us!"

The second woman turned to him. "The minute she gets a chance to run back to her rich friends, she forgets who took care of her!" She rounded on Laurel. "You owe me big-time, girl!"

"Renee Chapin, I presume?" Dan said dryly.

The angry woman looked toward him and paused in her diatribe. "That's right, sweetie."

Dan smiled. Renee's volatile personality coupled with Laurel's tightly coiled nerves had produced an explosion worth watching, but it was time to defuse the adversaries. "Was it necessary to run us off the road, Miss Chapin?"

"You coulda pulled over nice and easy."

Dan laughed. "Beautiful."

"Why, thank you."

He turned away, unable to hold in his amusement. She actually batted her false eyelashes at him. She couldn't know he was a cop. She wouldn't try something this blatant if she knew.

"What do you want?" Laurel screamed, and Dan realized Laurel still teetered on the brink.

"Yes, Ms. Chapin," he said, "what do you want?"

"Same thing I always wanted. Just grease my palm, honey."

"Good grief," Laurel said in disgust. "I told you and told you, I am not rich. My friends are not rich."

"Oh, right. You lived in a mansion back in Maine, and

you stay with friends out here who live pretty high. Doctors and such. You made me a promise, and I intend to see you keep it."

Laurel shook her head. "I never agreed to that. You threatened me, and you assumed I'd accept your terms, but I can't, even if I wanted to. I have nothing. Nothing. What don't you understand?"

"You got nice clothes."

"All at least two years old. I haven't had a new dress since my husband died. Renee, I can't help you. You've wasted the last month, chasing around after me—" Laurel stared at her. "How did you find me, anyway?"

Renee laughed. "You're not so hard to find. Some things are public record."

"Not my residence. That was confidential."

"Tell that to my parole officer." Renee shrugged.

"He got my address?"

"Just the town. I came out here and put my ear to the ground, so to speak."

"But—" Laurel stared at her.

"Then I found out I wasn't the only one looking for you. That cute guard at the hospital put me on to it."

"Troy?" Laurel asked.

"Whatever." Renee shook her head. "I don't know who those other guys are, but they look mean. They tracked you by your car, found your apartment and all. That's a guy thing, following a car."

"And how do women do it?" Dan asked. Laurel looked at him in surprise, but Dan had decided it was to their advantage to keep Renee talking. If he could stall her long enough, his hasty 911 call would pay dividends.

"I let them do the work and followed them, of course." She laughed. "You're just the cutest thing. I saw you twice at Laurel's place. The apartment, I mean. And you were packing up her things last week. Seemed personal."

A minivan came down the road. The driver slowed the vehicle and put down his window. "You folks all right?"

"Yeah, we're fine," Renee called. "Tow truck on the way."

The man nodded and was off. Laurel stared after him, but Renee picked up the conversation where she had left off.

"Once I learned those two jerks were on your tail, it wasn't hard to find you again."

"Sort of a modified *cherchez la femme*," Dan said with a half wink. "Very clever."

Laurel frowned at him.

"Oh, *cherchez la garbage*," Renee said. "I found you, didn't I?"

"How have you been living all this time if you have no money?" Laurel demanded.

Renee raised her shoulders slightly. "Best if you don't know." She smiled at Dan. "So, anyway, here we are. That truck ain't much, but I figure you've got a bank account, or at least some credit cards. You can let me have some honest money."

"Extortion isn't honest, Renee," Laurel said bitterly.

"Hey, hey, you don't want to talk like that!" Renee's head jerked suddenly, and her eyes lost their focus. Dan listened and was rewarded by the sound of an approaching siren.

"Don't tell me!" Renee glared at Dan.

He turned his palms upward in a gesture of innocence. "We didn't know it was a friend chasing us. What can I say?"

Renee swore as the patrol car pulled up behind her sedan and an officer got out.

Laurel stared at the approaching officer. Dan's on-duty partner, Jessica. Perfect. Maybe she could clean this up quickly.

"Hello, Dan," Jessica said. She looked at each of them in turn and nodded at Laurel. "Hello again."

Laurel nodded. Renee kept quiet but eyed Jessica warily.

"What's up, Dan?"

He gestured toward Renee. "This woman followed us out here and ran us off the road. Then she tried to extort money from us."

"Classic carjacking." Jessica took out her notebook.

"Hold it!" Renee cried. "We're old friends, Laurel and me."

"Really?" Jessica looked her over in distaste. "You should take some lessons in fashion from her. Although that blouse isn't bad."

Laurel choked back a laugh, wondering if Dan had told her about the stolen blouse.

"She really whacked your truck, Dan. Too bad. You've only had it since January."

Dan shook his head with a tight smile. "I'll have to call my insurance company."

Jessica ordered Renee to stand next to the squad car and patted her down, then put her into the backseat and went to the blue sedan. Dan approached Jessica and said something to her before returning to where Laurel was standing. "I tipped her off that Renee is a convicted felon."

Laurel nodded. "Dan, I'm sorry. I thought we'd made it. We were leaving all this mess behind us, and then there's Renee, hungry and loaded for bear."

He slipped his arm around her. "It's all right. Jess will sort it out. Come on, let's see if I can get the truck back up on the shoulder without a tow."

By the time the pickup was out of the field, Jessica had finished her preliminary work. She approached the truck, and Dan got out.

"Can you hold her?"

Jessica nodded. "You want to sign a complaint?"

"Not really. We were headed out of state."

"Well, she doesn't have a valid license."

"Give us two hours, Jess. Please?"

"I'll give you more than that. I called it in, and they're checking for outstanding warrants in Maine, but I can put her down for no license, no insurance and reckless driving. And her name doesn't match the registration. They're looking to see if the car's stolen. I can keep her tied up in red tape at least until morning."

"Great."

Jessica walked around the truck and stood by the passenger door. Laurel hesitated, then opened her window.

Jessica looked down at her for a long moment. "You're not on the run or anything, are you? I'll get in all kinds of trouble if I find out later you are."

"No. It's perfectly all right for me to be here."

Jessica nodded. "Your friend's a different story, though."

"She's harassed me. By the way, that's my blouse she's wearing. She stole it from me."

"Do you want it back?"

"No, thanks."

"Tell me something." Jessica looked past her and through the other window at Dan for a moment, then leaned closer to Laurel and said softly, "Do you love him?"

Laurel felt a sudden affinity for Jessica. "Yes."

Jessica nodded. "Well, he's my partner, and he's a good one. He'd better come back in one piece, in time for my wedding." She stood up. "All right, Dan. Best of luck."

Jessica turned back toward the patrol car just as a black Lincoln pulled over on the shoulder opposite Dan's truck and a man got out.

"Everything all right?" the man called.

"Under control," Jessica said, barely looking at him.

The man stepped forward and raised a pistol.

"Place your weapon on the ground, Officer."

THIRTEEN

Jessica stood still for a moment, and Dan was afraid she would draw her pistol. Instead she turned slowly to face the man.

"Nice and easy," he coaxed. "Don't do anything foolish."

A second man got out of the Lincoln and came to stand beside him.

Jessica eased her gun from the holster and stooped to lay it on the edge of the pavement.

Dan caught a faint sound behind him as Laurel stirred. He turned his head toward the truck and whispered, "Get down. Get low and don't move."

"You!" the gunman barked. "Step away from the truck."

Dan took a small step away from the pickup.

"Put your hands up, where I can see them."

Dan raised his hands to shoulder height.

"Where's Laurel Hatcher?" the second man asked.

"In the squad car," Jessica replied.

Dan clenched his teeth and was silent.

The gunman approached to within six feet of Jessica. "Give me the key."

She drew her key ring from her pocket and tossed it on the ground at his feet.

Dan watched, ready to act, but the man stepped back and kept the pistol leveled at Jessica, motioning for his companion to pick up the keys and Jessica's gun.

"Unlock the door," the first man said, and his friend went to the squad car, fumbling with the keys. He stuck Jessica's pistol in his belt and held up the key ring.

After several tense seconds, Jessica called, "The one with the square head."

A moment later, the man swung the door open and Renee stepped out.

"What are you jokers doing here?" Renee placed her hands on her hips. "Thanks for springing me, but I don't know as that's prudent just now."

The gunman glared at his companion. "That's not Laurel Hatcher, you imbecile."

"Watch it," Jessica said.

"I wasn't speaking to you, Officer," he said with exaggerated politeness. Then his face contorted and he yelled, "I never shot a *girl* cop before. Tell me now—where's the Hatcher woman?"

Jessica inhaled with a resigned air. "I thought she was Hatcher. They all lie, you know what I'm saying? Giving a false name to an—"

"Shut up!"

Renee marched past the man who had opened the car door and approached the gunman. "Temper, temper! You're apt to find yourself in a heap of trouble tonight. That cop is mean. She was going to run me in for nothing, and look at you! You're holding a gun on her."

The man swung toward Renee impatiently and Renee sprang like a cat on his arm, throwing her entire weight on the wrist that held the pistol. Jessica jumped to her aid, and Dan took a step as he drew his pistol from the shoulder holster under his jacket.

A shot rang out, but Dan was certain it went wild. Renee struggled with the man, trying to muscle him to the ground, with Jess in the thick of it.

The man nearest the patrol car reached for the gun in his belt, and Dan drew a bead on him. "Hands up!" he yelled.

The man stared at him, then complied. Dan strode to him and took Jessica's pistol. "Get in the car."

The man gaped at him, then meekly crawled into the backseat of the police car, and Dan slammed the door. He turned immediately toward the brawl.

"Jess, I've got you covered." He took another step, to where the gunman could see the weapon trained on him.

Jessica stood up slowly, and Dan handed over her pistol.

Renee rolled to a sitting position on the pavement. "Man! I broke a fingernail."

"Will you do the honors, Dan?" Jessica held out her handcuffs.

"Sure. You okay?"

"All but my bruised ego. Just cuff him and get out of here. I called for backup ten minutes ago."

"I'd better stay," Dan said.

"When you hear the siren, you skedaddle."

Renee stood up, grinning. "Sure. I'm a witness. I saw this cop subdue the both of them single-handed."

Jessica snorted. "Forget it. You're still going to jail,

sweetheart. But thanks. Just follow my lead when the backup gets here. These nice people drove off thirty seconds before these two goons showed up."

Dan handcuffed the prisoner and stood back. "Jess, I can stay," he repeated.

"No. Get her away from this. You've got at least twelve hours before the drama queen walks. I'll see to it. These other guys will have a longer stay, I'm sure."

Dan nodded. "Thanks."

He heard the approaching siren as he walked to the pickup.

Laurel was huddled down on the seat, her face bathed in tears.

"It's all right, Laurel. You can sit up now. Jessica's got things under control."

"What about Renee?"

"She'll behave. She can't get away—Jess has her car keys, and the backup is here."

He pulled onto the road. Laurel said nothing, but he heard her sniff once. When they were a good five miles from the scene of the crash, he pulled off at a scenic viewpoint and shut off the engine.

"Come here." Laurel slid over next to him, and he held her. "It's okay. Everything's okay."

"Oh, Danny, what else can happen?"

"Only good things."

She sighed. "I prayed."

He kissed her forehead. "Best thing you could do."

"But I really lost it back there with Renee."

"I wanted to know all your quirks."

"Yeah." She smiled shakily. "Are we heading for the interstate?"

"The airport first, I think. We can leave the truck in the long-term parking and get a rental. An everyday, blend-in sedan."

"Are you sure? That will be expensive."

"I think it's best. I'll send my keys to Jess or Owen. One of them can pick up the truck for me."

"I couldn't look when I heard the gun go off," she confessed.

"Good. I told you to stay down."

Laurel nodded. "I won't ask you how you got out of that one."

"A little finesse and some help from our friends." He squeezed her shoulders and started the truck. "I hate to say it, but you really do owe Renee one now. We all do."

As they drove across Ohio and part of Pennsylvania, they talked. Laurel began to droop as midnight approached. They stopped for a late supper at a truck stop, and after that she slept. Dan drove on, nearly to New York, before the adrenaline dissipated and he began to feel his fatigue.

Laurel stirred, and he said, "We'd better look for a hotel soon. I need some sleep." He squeezed her hand. "Want something to eat?"

"No, but I can drive for a while, if you want."

"We may as well rest."

They found a hotel near the highway, and Dan carried the briefcase full of documents into his room. He slept for ten hours and awoke feeling guilty, as though he'd neglected his responsibility, but when he called Laurel's room across the hall, she assured him all was well. He showered and shaved, and they went out for a meal.

They hit the road again, and Dan drove for eight hours into New Hampshire.

"Want to finish it tonight?" he asked her.

"There's no hurry. It's Saturday. We won't be able to see Jim tomorrow, anyway."

They found another motel, but this time Dan wasn't tired. Laurel came to his room and sat in an armchair while they watched the news. Dan sat on the edge of the bed, finding the arrangement a bit awkward. When the news was over, he took the remote and flipped through the channels available.

She stood up. "I think I'll go to bed."

"All right." He reached out to her tentatively. She grasped his hands and looked into his eyes, vulnerable and unsure.

"Let's just say good night."

He nodded. "Come on. I'll see you in."

He went out into the hallway with her and watched as she slid the card into the lock on her door.

"See you in the morning." She faced him with a smile that threatened to crumble.

The enormity of it struck him between the eyes. He'd just found her, and now he might lose her again, before he had the chance to declare his love for her. He reached for her, and she melted into his arms.

"It's going to work out," he whispered.

Far down the hall, a door opened. Laurel pried herself away from him and shrank into the doorway. "Good night, Danny."

Sunday dawned gray and miserable. Laurel met him in the hallway at seven, dressed in jeans and a blue pullover.

They ate the hotel's continental breakfast and set off north-ward. In spite of light traffic, the pounding rain slowed their progress.

That night they made two phone calls from a pay phone in Augusta, to Dan's parents and Judy. Dan insisted that he and Laurel go out for a real meal in a restaurant.

"Want to see a movie?" he asked when they returned to the hotel and entered the lobby, not wanting a repeat of the night before. He went to buy a newspaper from a vending machine by the desk so they could check the entertainment listings. As he approached it, the headline of the secondary article caught his eye, and he stopped in his tracks. *Hatcher retrial approaching. Attorneys prepare for second round.* A small photo of Laurel was surrounded by text.

He turned back, hoping to shield her from seeing it, but she stood beside him, staring at it.

"Might as well get one and see what the public thinks," she said.

"Are you sure you want to?"

"We've read everything else. I don't think anything can shock me now."

Dan kept the paper under his arm as they walked to her room. Laurel sat on the bed and opened it.

State prosecutors and defense attorneys are pre-paring their arguments for the retrial of Laurel Hatcher, 28, of Oakland, scheduled to begin June 19. Hatcher is accused of shooting her husband, Robert E. Hatcher, at their home two years ago. The case went to court last winter and ended in a mistrial.

Defense attorney James R. Hight, of Stevens,

Parker & Hight, in Waterville, said Saturday that he expects a good outcome for his client this time.

"We're entering new evidence on Mrs. Hatcher's behalf," Hight said. "My client has dealt with this for too long, and it's time the truth of her innocence becomes official."

However, Prosecuting Attorney Myron Jackson said the state will also offer new evidence in the case in an attempt to prove Hatcher's guilt.

Laurel pushed the paper at Dan. "You read the rest. I can't, but I know you need to."

She crossed the room to the window and stood looking out. Five minutes later, he shrugged, folding the paper.

"It's nothing, really. Just pretrial publicity. But it's made the public aware of it again. We'd better keep a low profile and not go out tonight. I'll call Jim first thing in the morning."

He shouldn't have insisted on the restaurant tonight, but he'd wanted to cheer her up and give her a sense of normalcy. At least no one had recognized her.

She walked to the window and peered out between the drapes, then turned and went to the desk, picked up the TV remote and clicked a few buttons.

"Sorry. I'm a little nervous."

"It's all right." Dan checked the TV listing. "Guess we don't want to watch anything tonight."

"What, all murder mysteries?"

He shrugged. "Nothing good. Let's play tic-tac-toe."

She laughed, but they sat opposite each other at the little table and played tic-tac-toe and the dot game for half an hour. Laurel was reckless, and Dan won time after time.

As he closed the last box on the dot game, she said, "I love you, Dan."

His heart tripped, and he looked into her solemn brown eyes and started to rise from the chair.

"No, stay right there." She pressed down on his arm gently.

He sat again, watching her, trying to tell her with his eyes that her words filled him with hope.

She nodded. "Just stay there, please. I don't trust you any closer."

He smiled. "I'll do whatever you say."

"Well, until Judy gets here, I say you have to keep your distance."

"Anything."

All things gray and miserable faded in importance. The rain, the newspaper article, his doubts about the future.

Thank you, God.

FOURTEEN

Jim Hight smiled as they entered his office in Waterville late Monday morning. He matched Laurel's description: tall and lanky, with a deceptively boyish look and an unruly head of dark hair.

"Laurel. So glad you had a safe trip."

"Thank you." Laurel shook his hand and presented Dan.

"Ryan," Hight said, sizing him up.

Dan measured him, too. For weeks he had weighed the idea of firing Hight and hiring a new attorney for Laurel, but now he felt they were allies. Dan thought he saw fight and persistence in Jim.

"We put out a few crumbs to the press this weekend," Hight began when they were seated, "just to start people thinking of you as a wronged woman."

"We saw it," Dan said. "What can we do in the next three weeks to move things along?"

"My investigator's been busy tracking down some of the character witnesses whose names Laurel gave me. These accusations by Renata Hatcher—that Laurel was a gold digger—may blow up in her face." He looked at Laurel. "I contacted your old minister, and his testimony may be helpful."

"Pastor Newman?"

"Yes. He remembered talking to you shortly before the murder. He'll testify that you were concerned about Bob and wanted the pastor to speak to him. Newman keeps records of counseling sessions and had made a note to set something up with Bob, but before he had a chance, Bob was killed. He doesn't for a minute think you did it, and he stressed that the session you had asked for wasn't for marriage counseling. He said your marriage was rock-solid, but you felt Bob was troubled by something at work."

Laurel nodded. "That's right. I hoped Pastor Newman could help Bob, since he wouldn't talk to me about it."

"Why didn't you bring this witness the last time?" Dan asked.

"Laurel didn't tell me any of this."

She raised her chin. "I didn't think it was important to the case. Besides, the pastor was on an extended trip when Bob was killed. I made some poor decisions then, and—well, I was just plain afraid."

"I think this witness will be helpful now," Hight said earnestly to Dan. "It shows Laurel's state of mind. She was trying to do things to help her marriage, not to end it."

Laurel sighed. "I'd like to see Pastor Newman."

"Can we?" Dan asked.

"I don't see why not. Best not to discuss his testimony, though."

Hight asked a secretary to call Newman while he went over the rest of the developments with Dan and Laurel.

"One more thing." The lawyer eyed Dan. "I know it's been two years, but we don't want any rumors flying about Mrs. Hatcher's current love life. I advise you to stay out of the public eye. Laurel, once the press knows you're in the area, they'll be after you, and if you're photographed with a man, it won't look good."

Dan nodded. "We'll try to keep out of the limelight."

"Even eating out or going to the grocery store together," Hight warned. "If Laurel were recognized…and heaven forbid anyone sees you going into a hotel room together."

"We'll make sure that doesn't happen," Dan said grimly.

"All right, I think that's it for now. Come by tomorrow, and we'll talk again." Hight stood up.

"I'd like to help you with the investigation if I can," Dan said.

Hight smiled. "I've got authorization to use you as an operative, for this case only, and I think we can work together. Relax today, and we'll discuss it tomorrow."

When they went into the outer office, the secretary said, "Mr. and Mrs. Newman would like you and Mr. Ryan to have lunch at their house."

Laurel looked eagerly at Dan. "I'd like that."

"Of course."

They went to the car, and Laurel directed him to the neighboring town of Oakland. On the main street, they passed an imposing square building with a sign that was hard to miss. She felt light-headed and looked away.

Dan squinted at the building. "Hatcher & Brody!"

"That's their main office."

As they approached the church, Laurel's nerves kicked

up even more. She'd known this would be difficult, but she was unprepared for overpowering grief.

Matthew and Louise Newman came from the parsonage before Dan had stopped the car.

"Laurel, dear!" Louise hugged Laurel as she stepped from the car.

"Mrs. Newman," Laurel choked. "It's so good to see you."

Dan shook hands with the couple. The Newmans drew them inside, and they sat at the kitchen table.

"I'm so glad your attorney called me," the pastor said. "If I'd known I could have helped you before, I'd have done anything. We prayed so hard for you."

"Matthew tried to find you after we read in the paper that you were released from jail," Louise said. "It was as if you'd vanished."

Laurel squeezed Louise's hand. "That was intentional. I didn't feel like I could come back here. Everyone assumed I did it."

"No, that's not so," the pastor said. "Louise and I never thought you could hurt Bob."

"We knew there was a problem," Louise agreed, "but you were trying to support him. Of course you didn't kill him!"

"Thank you," said Laurel. "I ought to have come to you, I guess. I got such negative reactions everywhere I went, and Bob's family turned totally against me. I wanted to get as far away from Oakland as I could."

"Where are you staying?" Mr. Newman asked.

"We have rooms at a hotel in Augusta."

"Come stay with us," Louise urged.

"Oh, no, we couldn't."

"Of course you could," Pastor Newman said. "The

children are all gone now. We have plenty of room for you both."

"My friend Judy is coming in a week, and we'll be staying with her," Laurel said.

"But this week?" Louise's eyes were bright with hope.

"We'd be· awfully close to the Hatcher family," Dan reminded them. "If she stays in Oakland, word will get around."

"Is that so awful?" the pastor asked.

"We don't want the press hounding her."

"We can be discreet," Louise insisted.

Laurel felt a new optimism. "Let's do it."

Dan touched the back of her sweater lightly. "All right, I'll run back to Augusta and check us both out. Would you like to visit the cemetery first?"

She drew a deep breath. "Yes. Thank you."

The Newmans walked with them down the shady gravel access road between rows of grave markers.

Robert E. Hatcher, beloved son. A bouquet of lemon lilies nestled at the base of the marker in the newer part of the cemetery.

"His parents put the stone there." Laurel stooped, touching the letters with her fingers.

"Mrs. Hatcher comes every Saturday and leaves flowers," Louise said.

Laurel stood abruptly, her hand at her lips, and stumbled down the gravel walk. Dan stared after her.

"I'll start lunch," Louise said. "She ought to have a bite before you go back to Augusta." She and Pastor Newman turned toward the house.

Dan walked after Laurel, not trying to catch up, just keeping her in sight. At the far edge of the cemetery, she sat down on a white iron bench, and he strolled toward her.

"May I sit down?" he asked.

"I don't think you're allowed. Someone might see us together."

Dan looked all around. No one was in sight, and he sat down and slipped his arm around her. Laurel took a deep, shaky breath, then with agonizing slowness lowered her head against his shoulder.

"It's going to be all right," he said.

"I don't like you staying in Oakland," Jim Hight said on Tuesday.

"We'll be careful," Dan said.

"Well, sunglasses won't be enough if word gets out." Hight opened a folder on his desk. "I think we're making progress. The district attorney is starting to question why Renata Hatcher ended up with her daughter-in-law's belongings, and I think the civil suit we filed against her and Wayne will go our way. They're also looking pretty hard at Hatcher & Brody's bidding procedures."

"It's about time," Dan said.

"I'd love to get someone into Hatcher & Brody to look around." Hight toyed with his pen. "Only trouble is, Wayne Hatcher knows my investigator, Ed Wilton." He picked up the back section of the morning's newspaper. "Of course, there is this."

He slid the paper across the desk, and Dan read the circled advertisement.

"It's perfect!"

"Thought that might interest you," Hight said smugly.

Laurel leaned over to read the notice.

"They're hiring security guards at H & B?" She looked from Jim to Dan.

Jim shrugged. "Guess they're feeling insecure with all this hullabaloo about the trial, and with the D.A. poking around."

The idea of Dan signing on to work for Wayne Hatcher and Jack Brody made her uneasy, but his eyes gleamed.

"It's better than I'd hoped. I can get inside their offices legally."

I can't let him! Someone at H & B killed Bob and hired two criminals to find me! She swallowed hard, knowing Dan's mind was made up.

Jim eyed Dan speculatively. "I assume you have genuine references."

Dan grinned. "Impeccable."

Laurel frowned and slumped back in her chair. "Don't you think that if there was something important in the office building they'd have found it by now? They wouldn't need to chase me around looking for it."

"Maybe." Jim looked at the paper again. "Which office was Bob's?"

"It's on the second floor, off the elevator to the right, last door on the left."

"We could go the safer route," Jim said. "I could ask for a warrant and search the office."

"Would the judge give it to you?" Dan asked.

"I don't know. I'd hate for Wayne Hatcher to get wind of it and start covering his tracks."

Dan stood. "Sounds like I'd better get over to Hatcher & Brody and apply for that job."

* * *

Dan began working for Hatcher & Brody the next night, taking the graveyard shift at the construction company's warehouse on the outskirts of Oakland. Laurel spent quiet mornings at the parsonage with Louise, while Dan slept in. Afternoons they rendezvoused with Hight and discussed the case, and in the evening they sat with the Newmans, enjoying their company. A couple of times Dan got his violin out and played hymns, with Louise accompanying him on the piano.

On Friday afternoon, he told Hight, "I haven't found anything suspicious yet. If I could just get moved to the office building!"

"Hang in there," said Hight.

Dan nodded. "I did volunteer for overtime. They're giving me shifts this weekend."

On Sunday, he was rewarded for his patience. The night man for the corporate offices called in sick.

"This is my chance," he told Hight on the phone.

"All right," Jim said. "Check out Bob's old office, for sure. And if you have the opportunity, we also need to know who handles the bids and who orders the materials for projects. Who ordered the inferior steel for the Maple Grove bridge, for instance."

When he came back to the parsonage shortly after seven in the morning, Dan was too excited to sleep.

"Let's go see Jim first."

At Hight's office, Dan reported that he had been able to do a quick investigation in the file room.

"Wayne Hatcher came in just before midnight and stayed in his office for about an hour. But after he left, I found the materials orders for the latest project. The project manager's signature and Jack Brody's are on them."

"Interesting," said Jim. "I wonder if he signed the order for the bridge."

"If they put me back in there, I'll try to locate the older records," Dan said. "They may all be computerized. If I had time to sit down at the computer, I could get into their financial and personnel records."

"How about bids?" Jim asked.

"They've submitted bids on four projects this year, and got two. The main competitor on both the ones they landed was Simon Brothers."

"What about the others?"

"Simon Brothers got a contract for a school addition in Bangor, and another company got one to take out a dam on the Sebasticook River. Simon didn't bid on that one."

"You think Hatcher & Brody could have had the school contract if they'd wanted it?"

Dan shrugged. "I couldn't say. They're busy enough without it. But they might have bid on it just to keep Simon Brothers from making more allegations of bid-fixing."

"They must have a mole in Simon Brothers." Jim leaned back in his chair. "Who would handle the bids?"

"The estimator and the project manager. The company president would have to give final approval, I'd think," said Dan.

"No, I mean who actually held the bid in his hands after the numbers were decided on."

Dan's eyes narrowed. "A secretary? Someone has to type it up and mail it."

"I'll put Wilton on it," Jim said. "We'll see if we can

find out who in Simon Brothers' office would have physical access to a bid between the boardroom and the opening."

"You think H & B is paying someone at Simon Brothers?" Laurel asked.

"Could be. But would it be an official payment, on the books?" Jim asked. "Dan, if you can get in the offices again, look for large payments, especially even sums, to an individual."

"Right. Oh, and guess who's got Bob's old office."

Jim shrugged.

"Jack Brody."

Laurel frowned. "He used to be down the hall next to Wayne."

"Guess he liked Bob's corner view better."

Jim sighed. "Let's hope they put you in the office building again."

"If they do," Dan said, "I have a feeling I'm on the brink of finding something that will prove once and for all that Laurel is innocent."

FIFTEEN

The Tuesday before the trial began, Dan was again assigned as watchman at the corporate office building. He made his rounds alone at an even pace, the way he had at the hospital.

This might be his last chance to search the files, he realized. Judy had arrived the day before, and he and Laurel had joined her at a modest cottage on the shore of Messalonskee Lake. They were enjoying the peaceful days on the water, but the opening day of the trial loomed before them, giving Dan an urgency when he made his rounds at Hatcher & Brody.

As he checked the offices on the second floor, his excitement grew. No one worked late tonight, and all the rooms were dark.

He punched the clock outside Bob's old office and listened to be sure no one else was present, then went in and turned on his penlight. *Jack Brody, Vice President of Operations,* the name plaque on the walnut desk read. Jack kept a neat desk, with only the plaque and an in-and-out tray on the surface.

Dan knew he needed to find proof that Brody knew

about the switch on the bridge materials, although he doubted that that in itself would be enough to cause Jack to kill his nephew. And Brody's alibi for the day of the murder seemed ironclad—he and his girlfriend attended a field day in Rockland, and a hundred people could vouch for them. So whatever Dan found regarding the fraudulent bidding process wouldn't directly solve the murder, but he was convinced it was somehow related to Bob Hatcher's death.

Dan checked each desk drawer quickly then turned to a file cabinet in the corner. If he found nothing significant there, he would make another round of the building and spend a few extra minutes in the file room to look for the older project files.

On a whim, he flipped through the folders to *M*—Maple Grove—and smiled. A thick folder bore the title. He took it to the desk and spread out the contents.

As he picked out an invoice from a steel beam distribution company in New Jersey, he heard the elevator door open.

Dan froze for an instant and then shoved the papers back into the folder, his heart hammering. A light came on in the hallway. No time to put the file back in its proper place. He slid open the top center desk drawer and was closing it on the folder when the office door swung open and the light came on.

"Who in blazes are you?"

Jack Brody's graying blond hair was tousled, and his flashing eyes didn't quite focus. Dan suspected he'd had a few drinks.

"I'm the night watchman, sir."

"What are doing in my office?"

"I was making my rounds, sir."

His glance flicked to the halfway open file drawer, then back to Dan's face. "Oh, you were, were you?"

"Yes, sir." Brody's smile told Dan that he didn't believe a word.

"When did we hire you?" Brody weaved forward and sat on the corner of the desk.

Dan stepped back a pace. "About two weeks ago, sir."

"Simon planted you here."

"No, sir."

"You're lying."

"I'm not. I saw your ad in the—"

"Piffle." He said the *F*'s slowly and carefully.

Dan swallowed. Jack Brody had at least forty pounds on Dan, but still he thought he could subdue the older man if he had to.

"What's your name?"

"Dan Ryan, sir."

"Where do you live?"

"I'm staying in Belgrade right now."

"Who's paying you?"

"Hatcher & Brody, sir."

"Besides us, idiot. Who sent you here?"

Dan took a deep, careful breath. "Nobody else is paying me to be here, Mr. Brody."

"So you just took it upon yourself to come snoop through our private offices while you were on duty."

Dan was silent, unable to come up with a truthful reply that wouldn't further entangle him.

"Come on, you're neglecting your job to come in here and look at private papers. Do you think I'm stupid?"

Dan watched, fascinated, as Brody reached inside his blazer. He knew, before he saw it, what would be in Brody's hand when he brought it out, though the compact pistol hadn't made much of a bulge under the jacket. Dan stared at it. He had been shot at once, when he responded to an armed robbery, but he'd been twenty yards away, and the man had missed. He was scarcely a yard away from Jack Brody.

But Brody's hand shook.

"Pick up the phone," Brody said.

Dan reached for the receiver, without taking his eyes from the big man's face.

"Call the cops."

"But, sir—"

"Security guards aren't allowed to rifle their employers' files and steal secret papers. You're going to do time, Ryan. If you think your *other* employer will bail you out, forget it. Simon won't admit he sent you to spy on us. You can tell any little story you want, but no one will believe you."

Dan held his gaze, his mind whirling.

"Go on, dial," Brody snarled. "It's 911, or are you too stupid to know that?"

Dan pushed the buttons and held the receiver to his ear.

"Do you have an emergency?"

"Yes, this is Dan Ryan. I'm the security guard at Hatcher & Brody. Could you send an officer over here to our corporate offices, please? We've apprehended someone."

"Hold on."

Brody smiled. "You're smooth, Ryan. Hang up."

Dan opened his mouth, then closed it. He hung up on the dispatcher.

"Come on." Brody stood and wiggled the gun back and forth. "Let's go down to the lobby and wait for the nice policemen." His body swayed.

Dan walked slowly, wondering if Jim Hight would be able to straighten this out with the local police. He headed for the elevator, but Brody stopped him.

"Take the stairs. I like that story you told 911 about an intruder. Maybe the burglar got the jump on you after you made the call. See, that way you wouldn't be able to tell the cops anything, would you, now?"

"You said they wouldn't believe me anyway." Dan hesitated at the top of the open stairway.

"Well, I've been thinking on it. We've taken a lot of flak on our business practices lately. Maybe I can't afford to let you tell your story after all. Yes, this will be better. I think…about…halfway down." Brody looked past him at the stairs. "Then turn around and face me."

SIXTEEN

A vision of his own body spread-eagled on the stairs in a pool of blood, the way Bob's had been, crossed Dan's mind. That would be too much for Laurel.

Dear God, help me!

He whirled and seized Brody's wrist, slamming it down forcefully on the stair rail. The gun flew over the edge and clattered to the floor below. Brody gasped and lunged for Dan's throat, but Dan stepped back and kicked as hard as he could, and the bigger man flew backward down the stairs. Dan scrambled after him. Brody lay gasping, one hand groping at his chest. Dan knelt and patted Brody's pockets, his waistline and under his arms for more weapons.

A blue light flashed over the walls of the lobby below. Dan stepped carefully over Brody and ran down to open the door.

"You the man who called?"

"Yes, sir, Dan Ryan."

"Where's your subject?"

"On the stairs."

Dan leaned against the door frame, breathing hard, as

the officer dashed across the lobby. A second patrol car pulled up in front of the building.

"This is Jack Brody," the officer on the stairs called.

"Yes, sir."

"He and his brother-in-law own this place. He's not an intruder."

"No, sir, I never said he was. He tried to shoot me. The gun's down there." Dan pointed to where Brody's pistol lay in the shadows below the stairway.

The second officer came warily through the door.

"What happened?"

"Call an ambulance for Mr. Brody," his buddy yelled. "He's having trouble breathing."

They kept Dan at the police station for three hours after Jack Brody was put in the ambulance. He used his one phone call to rouse Jim, rather than alarm Laurel and Judy.

Hight arrived soon after, but the Oakland police were reluctant to believe Dan was an Ohio patrol officer moonlighting as a private investigator, even though Jim showed them a copy of the state's permission for him to use Dan as a temporary investigator. Jim ended up calling Laurel at 2:00 a.m. and asking her to bring Dan's Ohio license. The patrol sergeant took the papers and disappeared.

"There's still the matter of you breaking into Brody's office," investigating officer Philbrook said.

"I didn't break in. I'm on Hatcher & Brody's payroll, and I had a master key to the offices. I'm a security guard." Dan tried to be patient. Laurel and Judy stood by, Judy avidly following matters, Laurel pale and shaky.

"Brody said you stole something from his desk."

"No, sir. I was making my rounds of the offices when he came in."

"He also said you were going through a file cabinet," Philbrook insisted. "That's not part of the job."

Dan looked toward Jim.

"I need a moment alone with my client," Jim said.

Philbrook sighed and took Laurel and Judy out of the room.

"Please tell me you found something," Jim whispered.

"Papers about the investigation into the bridge failure, that's all."

"You didn't take anything?"

"No."

Jim nodded. "All right, I'll have you out of here in ten minutes. It didn't work out, that's all." He went to the door and returned with Philbrook and the patrol sergeant. "Mr. Ryan will make a complete statement now. He had a right to be there. Hatcher & Brody paid him to check all the offices."

"Not to snoop in the executives' desks."

"He didn't take anything, and he didn't make any copies or photos."

"Let him go," the sergeant said from the doorway.

Jim Hight looked at the man's name tag. "Thank you, Sergeant. Theriault."

"I've been on the phone with a fellow in Ohio." Theriault looked squarely at Dan. "You know a Lieutenant Powers?"

"Yes, sir, very well."

"He says you're all right. You think Brody would have shot you?"

"Yes, sir, he told me as much."

"You'll sign a complaint to that effect?"

"Certainly."

Theriault turned to Philbrook. "Release him. You got a man at the hospital with Brody?"

"Yes, sir."

"Get over there and charge Brody with attempted murder. If that won't stick, we'll get him for carrying a concealed weapon without a permit. I want him in custody until the D.A. has a chance to sort this thing out."

"But, sir—"

"But nothing. The Hatcher trial is coming right up. We don't want anything underhanded going on that will keep Mrs. Hatcher from getting a fair trial, do we?"

"No, sir," said Philbrook.

Theriault nodded. "As for you, Ryan, I suggest you resign your job at H & B immediately."

"Yes, sir."

Dan followed the officers out to the duty room and went to Laurel. "Are you all right?" He slipped his arm around her as she drew a deep, shuddering breath.

"You're Laurel Hatcher," Theriault said.

"Y-yes."

Dan pulled a chair out quickly, afraid she would collapse. "Sit down, sweetheart."

"No, I'll be all right. I just need some fresh air."

"Can we go?" Jim asked.

"Yes," Theriault replied. "We may want to talk to Ryan again, but I think that's it for now."

"Thank you." Dan extended his hand to Theriault. "I'll be at the cottage I told you about."

Theriault nodded and smiled at Laurel. The smile changed his features from merciless authority to pleasant goodwill. "Best of luck, Mrs. Hatcher. Your husband was a good man. A lot of us are rooting for you."

Later that day, Dan stopped the car across the street from the majestic Queen Anne house that had once been Laurel's home. She struggled against the tide of memories, but gave up. She couldn't hold them back. Maybe she could sort them and retain only the happy ones.

The three-story house had four kinds of decorative shingles and carved brackets under the eaves. The porch wrapped around the front and two sides, beneath a round tower and gabled roof. The blocks of the foundation had designs embossed on the concrete, and a stained glass window hung between stories where the stairs turned.

"Wow," Dan said at last.

"Yeah. It's a great house." It was hard not to imagine Bob coming down the steps to greet her. Laurel sent up a fractured prayer of thanks for the four years she'd had him. She had expected the house to repel her. Instead, she felt drawn to it. She got out of the car and walked across the street, sensing Dan at her elbow. They stood at the edge of the lawn, under the new green leaves of the big maple. A scooter and a soccer ball lay on the grass.

"I'm glad a family lives here now," she said through her tears. "It's a house that ought to have children in it."

"I could never give you a house like that."

"I don't need a house like that," she said.

Dan stared at the tower. "Did you have a telescope up there?"

"No. Do you like astronomy? I thought you told me everything."

He chuckled. "Everything but that, I guess. Do you want to go in?"

"I...don't think so."

"You sure?"

When she hesitated, he went up the walk, mounted the porch and rang the doorbell.

Drawing a breath was almost painful. Did she really want to meet the new owners of the house she and Bob had made their own? What if they said cruel things? The door opened, and a blond woman greeted Dan. Laurel turned her face away and waited for him to come back.

A moment later, he hurried toward her.

"Come on. The lady is really nice. She said you can come in and look around."

"I'm not sure...." Laurel gulped and took a step. Dan slipped his arm around her, and they strolled toward the house.

"I'm Gretchen Dufour," the woman said. "My husband's an eye surgeon, and we moved here from Pennsylvania. Please come in."

Laurel grasped her offered hand and stepped into the foyer. At once she noted a different light fixture hanging overhead, but the wallpaper she had picked out five years ago remained unscathed.

"You're the former owner?" Gretchen asked. "Please forgive me, but the neighbors told us there was...a death in this house. And I've read things in the papers. I'm glad you came back, Mrs. Hatcher."

"Thank you." Laurel glanced at Dan and read encouragement in his expression. Of course. He'd told Gretchen that Laurel was here to prove her innocence. She turned back to Gretchen. "My husband was killed here. I hope that doesn't bother you. I mean, I hope it doesn't make you not want to live here. It's a fantastic house."

"Oh, we love it. But I haven't told the children." Gretchen smiled. "Say, could I get you folks a glass of iced tea? My kids are at school. I was working on a project, but I could use a break."

Laurel raised her eyebrows at Dan. They were bending Jim's rules for sure.

Dan shrugged. "If you're comfortable."

The new owners had remodeled the kitchen, with new oak cabinets and sleek steel appliances. Laurel and Dan sat at a round table near the patio door, looking out on the backyard where Laurel used to set up her easel on sunny days.

"The kitchen looks great," she said when Gretchen brought their glasses.

"Thanks. The house was empty when we bought it. Not even any curtains. In fact, in the entry, there were wires dangling, like someone had removed the chandelier and not replaced it."

Renata. She always loved that.

Laurel forced a smile. "My…friend and I…" She glanced at Dan. "We wondered if you'd found anything in the house, but I guess not."

Dan cocked one eyebrow, but didn't contradict her.

"No, it was stark naked. Not one stick of furniture. But that made it easy to do the changes we wanted. If you'd like, I'll take you upstairs and show you what we've done there. New carpets. I've made Julianne's room up like a princess bower."

Laurel wasn't sure she wanted to see the stairs, or the bedroom she and Bob had shared, but she smiled. "How old is she?"

"Seven." Gretchen sipped her tea. "The only traces we found of the previous owners were a few splotches of paint on the floor in the tower—"

"My fault," Laurel said.

"—and an old key in the basement."

Dan sat up. "A key?"

"Yes. In one of those magnetic cases. You know—the kind you keep under your car bumper, in case you get locked out."

Dan nodded. "In the basement, you say?"

Gretchen stood and went to the counter. "Tim found it when he was poking around there with the technician who came to clean the furnace last fall. What did I do with it? He said the case was stuck to the back of the furnace." She opened a drawer.

Dan whispered to Laurel, "Do you know anything about that?"

She shook her head.

"It's kind of a funny-looking key. He said it wasn't a car key." Gretchen opened another drawer. "Ha! There it is."

She returned to the table and held out a small, flat container. Laurel let Dan take it and slide it open.

A gleam flickered in his eyes, and Laurel sat forward. "What is it?"

Dan dumped the oddly shaped key into the palm of his hand.

"Mrs. Dufour, I believe this belonged to Laurel's husband. May we take it?"

"I guess so. It's no good to us. Would you folks like to see the rest of the house now?"

Laurel started to decline, but Dan beat her to it.

"I'm sorry, but we need to leave. You've been very kind."

Gretchen followed them through the foyer and onto the porch, a frown wrinkling her brow.

"Thank you," Laurel said.

"You're welcome. And I'm very sorry about your husband."

Laurel took one last glance around the entry. No longings or regrets waylaid her. "We had good times in this house, and I hope you and your family do, too."

They drove straight to Jim's office. The secretary showed them in, and Dan produced the key.

"What's this?" Jim asked.

"Unless I miss my guess, it's the key to a safe-deposit box."

Jim took it and squinted at it. "BNE. Bank of New England?"

"Bob and I had accounts at the Oakland branch." Laurel couldn't keep her voice steady. Dan reached for her hand and gave it a reassuring squeeze.

"The new owners of Laurel and Bob's old house found it hidden in the basement."

"Well, well."

"Do you think that's what the men chasing me were looking for?" Laurel asked.

Jim reached for his phone. "Let's not jump to conclusions. It may have nothing to do with your case. It could have been there before you and Bob moved in. Don't you think Bob would have told you about it if it were his?"

She blew out a long breath and sank into a chair. "I honestly don't know."

"He wanted to protect her from what was going on at work," Dan said.

Jim frowned. "If the men pursuing Laurel were after this, how did they know it existed?"

Laurel sat back in silence. That troubled her, too.

"Well, we're closer to solving this thing than we were this morning," Jim said. "My investigator has narrowed the suspects among Simon Brothers' employees down to three: a secretary, a file clerk and Arthur Simon's personal assistant. We're doing background checks on them to see if we can find a link. Personally, I like the assistant for this. She's more likely to handle sensitive material like that.

"Great." Dan stood up. "Are you going to call the bank?"

"Yes. I'll set up an appointment with the bank manager and go over to discuss this with him in person. They can check the records to see who held the box this key goes to. I doubt Laurel's name is on it, because she'd have had to sign when the box was rented. If it's not, but Bob's name is, we'll need a warrant to access the contents."

That evening, Dan rowed Laurel to the middle of the lake. The moon rose, three quarters full, and they sat in its soft glow, looking across the water at the sharper dots of cottage lights sprinkled along the far shore. The flat surface of the lake looked so solid in the moonlight that Laurel felt she could step over the side and walk back to the dock.

"I want to ask you something," Dan said. "Don't answer right away, just think about it."

She lowered her lashes. "What is it?"

"Will you marry me when the trial is over?"

She sat on the stern seat, looking at him. He had shipped the oars and was watching her, his earnest gaze full of love.

"Dan, I—"

"Don't answer yet. Please. At least give me a few minutes to hope."

His solemn voice brought Laurel a wave of remorse. The last thing she wanted to do was to hurt him again.

"I told you, I can't promise. If things go wrong, I can't—"

"If things go wrong, we'll make a new plan. Laurel, I love you so much, and I know you feel the same way about me." He grasped her hand and brought it to his lips. "We belong together, so please think about it."

She *had* thought about it, many times. Lifting her eyes to the starlit sky, she knew what she wanted. More than anything, she wanted a future with Dan, an unpretentious house…and gray-eyed babies.

Dear God, please, give us a chance.

"All right," she said, "I'm thinking about it. I'll give you my answer when the trial is over."

He moved carefully from the middle seat to the stern and sat down beside her, drawing her into his arms in one fluid motion and kissing her with all the hope she had handed him in the moonlight.

On Friday Jim came to the cottage with news.

"The safe-deposit box was opened this morning in the presence of the district attorney and myself. It was full of documents," he told Dan and Laurel.

"What kind of documents?" Laurel asked.

"Copies of contracts and estimates from H & B, all dated within the last year of Bob's life."

Laurel swallowed hard. "What did they tell you?"

"I haven't had time to read everything yet, but Jack Brody is the one who signed off on all the materials for the Maple Grove Bridge. I'm not sure Wayne Hatcher knew about the steel switch. It looks to me like it was all Brody's idea. He saw they'd cut it too close on the bid and ordered the inferior stock. But I don't know why Hatcher is keeping him on in the firm, now that he knows. It's costing him plenty to redo that job."

"Don't forget, Jack is Renata's brother," said Dan.

"She and Jack are very close," Laurel agreed. "And she wears the pants. I don't think she'd let Wayne boot Jack out of the company, even if he pulled a stunt like that."

Jim nodded. "We also learned H & B put in their bid on the bridge at the last minute. They had prepared a proposal, but they held it until the morning the bids were due. Then Brody revised it, lowering their bid a quarter of a million."

Dan whistled. "He had to know what Simon was proposing."

"I think so."

"And Bob found out how they were doing it," Laurel said.

Dan nodded. "He must have. The way I see it, he confronted his uncle. Told him he had this evidence, but not where he was hiding it."

"But Jack couldn't have killed him," Laurel reminded him. "He has an airtight alibi."

Jim waved his hand in dismissal. "He hired it done."

Laurel swallowed. Which was worse, a family member pulling the trigger, or a hired assassin?

"Oakland Limited seems to be involved in the bridge project, too," Jim said.

"What's that?" Dan asked.

"It's a concrete company," Laurel said immediately. "H & B subcontracted to them a lot."

"So, if H & B got a fat contract, Oakland Limited would profit, as well?"

"I suppose."

Jim nodded. "We found records of payments to them before and during the bridge construction."

"Is that significant?" Laurel shook her head doubtfully. "They gave Larry a lot of business."

Dan did a double take. "Larry, as in Larry *Let's-quit-the-golf-game-I-have-a-headache* Mason?"

Laurel stared at Dan. "You don't think—"

"I'm willing to think anything at this point."

She turned to Jim. "Do you think Larry Mason is mixed up in the underbidding?"

Jim raised his eyebrows. "I have an open mind."

The last few days before the trial crawled by. Laurel wished she knew if the state police had moved yet on the material found in Bob's cache, and if any arrests had been made. No hint of the potential scandal made the local news broadcasts.

Dan explained that if his department in Ohio handled a case of conspiracy and industrial espionage, the detectives would move slowly, even if it were connected to a two-year-old murder. They would perform their own investigation, not just accept at face value what an attorney's private investigators handed them. It might be weeks before Jack Brody and Larry Mason faced charges. And so Laurel waited for the trial to begin.

She spent a quiet hour on the dock Saturday morning, while Judy made a trip into town for groceries. Her helplessness and frustration grew as she mulled over what they knew. When Judy returned, she brought sandwiches and iced tea to the dock and sat on the edge, dangling her bare feet in the water.

"Any news?"

"No. Dan's still sleeping, and Jim hasn't called."

"Laurel, I know this man Larry was supposed to be Bob's friend, but…"

"I know," she groaned. "I keep thinking about what he said on the witness stand, about me being a better shot than him. And I was!"

"He knew about the gun."

"Yes. He was at our house all the time. He knew exactly where Bob kept it."

"Could Larry have done it?"

"He picked Bob up that morning, before I left for Bangor. During their golf game, he claimed he had a headache, and they drove to our house. Maybe Bob offered him some aspirin. Anyhow, he went in the house with Bob. He didn't need an excuse. He was a frequent guest, and he and Tina had a key to our house. It wouldn't matter if he left fingerprints around the house, except for on the murder weapon."

Judy kicked up a little spray of water. "But if they were so close, why would this Larry want to kill Bob?"

Laurel shrugged. "It's all tangled up in the bidding and the bridge project. I just hope what they found in Bob's safe-deposit box will answer all the questions."

Judy looked toward the cottage, and Laurel followed her gaze. Dan was coming down the path.

"Morning, ladies."

"You look more rested," Judy said.

"Thanks. I think I'm catching up, finally." He sat down in a deck chair next to Laurel. "I just spoke to Lieutenant Powers. He told me Jessica Alton has been trying to get a message to me."

Laurel raised her eyebrows. What could Jessica be dying to tell Dan?

He smiled and took her hand. "It may ease your mind a bit. Remember the two guys chasing you in Ohio?"

"How could we forget?" Judy asked.

"Well, one of them talked. Jack Brody hired them to find you, Laurel. Seems the bank notified Bob's parents' attorney that they had a safe-deposit box in Bob's name and it should be considered part of the estate."

"What does that have to do with Laurel?" Judy asked.

"They figured she had the key."

"Could they have opened it even if they had it, with the estate tied up in court?" Laurel asked.

"Maybe not, but I figure it this way. Wayne was upset, because by the time they learned about the box, his company was in trouble, thanks to Jack."

Laurel nodded. "And Renata must have told Jack about the key."

"Sure. Jack would want to see what was in there, not only before the lawyer did, but maybe before Wayne did, too."

"So he set the bloodhounds on you." Judy grimaced. "Good old Uncle Jack."

"He's not doing so well," Dan said with a frown. "He had a massive heart attack."

"Don't blame yourself," Judy warned him. "He would have killed you, and you know it."

"Yes, and the men he hired to find the evidence tried to kill Laurel and me in Ohio. If Jack survives, he can be charged with murder-for-hire. And maybe Renata can, too, as an accessory."

Laurel's stomach roiled, and she touched his arm. "Let's get through this trial first, okay?"

Dan squeezed her hand. "You've got it. We'll let the police worry about the rest of it now."

SEVENTEEN

On Saturday, they held their final pretrial conference with Jim Hight.

"Wear something feminine, but not too fancy," Jim told Laurel. "And don't wear your hair like that."

Laurel put a hand to her temple.

"What's wrong with it?" Dan asked. Judy had French-braided Laurel's hair that morning, and he thought it looked good.

"We want a softer image, more sympathetic," Jim said. "Grieving widow wrongly accused, easily hurt. Loose hair, full skirt, no cleavage."

"I get the picture," Laurel said acidly.

"Here's the scoop." Jim opened a folder. "My investigator found the link."

"What link?" Laurel demanded.

"Arthur Simon's personal assistant. She's Larry Mason's cousin."

"So Larry got his cousin to peek at the bids for him?" Laurel asked. "I can't believe this."

"And paid her well for it. He passed the information on

to Brody. Brody made the final bid for H & B, so H & B got the contract…and Larry got a hefty kickback."

"Bob knew Jack was doing it, but he didn't know how," Dan said.

"If he'd known Larry was in on it, he wouldn't have been playing golf with him." Laurel shook her head.

"I think you're right," Dan agreed. "Bob threatened to expose Jack, and Jack was scared. Getting hit with big penalties for the materials scam was one thing, but Brody knew he could go to prison for cheating on the bids. He and Larry and the assistant would all be charged with conspiracy. Maybe Wayne Hatcher, too. Jack counted on Larry to fix it."

"Oh, no," Laurel breathed. "Uncle Jack wouldn't want Larry to kill Bob and frame me."

"Jack probably didn't know Larry would shoot him," Dan said. "He might have told him to take care of things and expected him to reason with Bob. Or, if that failed, threaten him."

Laurel shuddered.

"Bob didn't scare easily," Jim said. "Anyway, we're turning all the information over to the district attorney today. We've got proof Larry was paying off his cousin, and she's likely to confess. We've also got the records of H & B's payments to Mason's company. There's more money there than his concrete work accounts for." Jim tossed the file folder on his desk. "So relax, have a quiet Sunday and be on time at the courthouse Monday morning."

"We're going to church tomorrow," Laurel said.

Jim shrugged. "Suit yourself. It's so close now, it can't hurt much. But no hand-holding in public, and under no circumstances do you talk to reporters."

* * *

Laurel sat tensely quiet through the jury selection Monday morning. The imposing courtroom, with its arched vault and long, red-draped windows. intimidated her. Dark portraits of justices from a century ago stared down dispassionately from their gilded frames high on the walls. Dan's father would love to work with the wide cherry boards of the wainscoting.

Laurel never spoke as Jim Hight questioned potential jurors in his turn, disqualifying a few and accepting others. Dan and Judy were not allowed in the courtroom during the process. By noon, the twelve jurors and three alternates had been chosen. Jim drove her to the appointed meeting place, a restaurant a few blocks from the courthouse.

"It's all set," Jim told Dan as they took their menus. "The session opens at one."

"Good!" said Dan. "Let's get it over with."

"Don't sit right behind us, where the family sits. I don't want reporters asking who you are, Ryan, and I don't want the jurors making the romantic connection. It still might matter."

"Even with the new evidence?" Judy asked.

"A jury trial ain't over till it's over," Jim said.

Dan squeezed Laurel's hand under the table.

Jim lowered his voice. "I did my best this morning to have the case dismissed. The prosecutor and I met with Judge Hurst in his chambers early. I took a copy of the statement Jack Brody made to the police. His doctor told him he may not make it, and he came clean. He admitted trying to kill Dan because he didn't want Dan to expose him. But His Honor says that's not enough to throw this trial out."

Laurel listened attentively, wondering whether to muster hope from the turn of events.

"Come on, it's the motive," Dan said.

Hight shook his head. "Hurst says that doesn't prove that the bid-fixing is directly related to the murder, and Jack has an alibi for that, so we have to proceed. If Brody had admitted to killing Bob or conspiring to kill him, that would be another story, but as it is—well, I can introduce this bidding mess during direct examination, but I'll have to be careful." He opened his briefcase on the corner of the table and pulled out a manila folder. "Take a look at this, Ryan. Sergeant Theriault brought it over to my office this morning."

"What is it?" Laurel asked, looking over Dan's shoulder as he opened the folder.

"It's a copy of the original report made the day of the murder by the two officers who went to your house. I skimmed it, but I didn't see anything new."

Dan began reading the papers.

A man in a suit stepped up to their table. "Excuse me, Mr. Hight, I'm with the *Kennebec Journal*. May I ask you a few questions?"

"Oh, great!" Jim stood up and put his long, muscular body between Laurel and the reporter. "My client would like to have a quiet lunch here, if you don't mind."

"But, sir, if you'd just give me a few minutes—"

"I'll give you this—Laurel Hatcher is innocent. Please leave us alone."

"Come on." Dan scooped up the folder and led Judy and Laurel quickly away from the table.

"What about Jim?" Laurel asked as they hurried to the car.

"He can fend for himself. We'll catch up with him at the courthouse."

Dan drove to a deli and left the two women in the car while he ran inside for sandwiches and cold drinks.

Laurel had done everything they'd told her to: worn a full, gray-blue skirt and a spotless white blouse, fixed her hair in soft, flowing waves, put on her wedding ring. But she couldn't eat.

Dan smiled sympathetically at her and read the police report while he ate his sandwich.

On the way back to the courthouse they passed the Kennebec County Jail, with its cold granite walls and the exercise yard beside it, with rolls of coiled razor wire along the top of the high fence. Laurel took a shaky breath and turned away.

Jim joined them in an anteroom across the hall from the courtroom.

"Find anything in that police report?"

"Two neighbors saw Larry's car at the Hatchers' house that day," Dan said. "One fits the time Larry says he dropped Bob off...the other thought it was later."

"Yeah, we went through all that last time."

"Can somebody talk to those neighbors again, Jim? They're on your witness list, but you decided not to call them."

"Because Larry admits being at the Hatchers' that morning."

Dan frowned. "The time element bothers me. The autopsy puts the time of death as between 1:00 and 2:00 p.m."

"So?"

"So one neighbor said he saw the car there at one-fifteen."

Jim eyed him carefully. "Do you want to skip the opening session and go talk to them? It probably won't do any good."

Dan looked at Laurel. She wanted him there in the courtroom, but this was the only lead they had come up with. If Bob's carefully compiled documentation of the fraudulent bidding wasn't enough to exonerate her, they had to follow up any other possibility, no matter how remote. Time was running out.

"The neighbors are all we've got," he said. "Do you mind?"

"Go ahead," she said. "Judy will be here."

Laurel shivered as she entered the courtroom beside her lawyer. There had been no chance to have a last, private word with Dan, no sustaining embrace, no encouraging squeeze of the hand.

In his opening statement the state's prosecuting attorney, Myron Jackson, described Laurel to the jury as a discontented young wife. She had tried to persuade her husband to leave his father's business, abandon his family and move with her to another state. When Bob refused, Laurel grew resentful. She fought with her husband in front of his family and contemplated divorce. In the end, after an argument in their home, she killed him.

Laurel blanched as the diatribe went on. She could almost hear Renata delivering the litany. She stared straight ahead, at the court recorder who clacked on and on, taking down the words.

Jim's opening statement presented a different picture of Laurel. She was a bereaved woman wronged by her in-laws, her friends and the state of Maine. He recounted the hardships she had suffered since her husband's death.

"And we will show," he declared to the jury, "that Laurel Wilson Hatcher did not kill her husband. She loved her husband. She knew he was in some kind of danger, and she wanted to help him. She certainly didn't want him dead. And the state cannot prove that she did. But we will show that someone else wanted him dead, someone who saw Bob Hatcher as a threat."

The state began calling its witnesses. The medical examiner was first. His detailed account of the cause of death brought back the vivid memories Laurel had tried so hard to suppress. She had known it would be like this, but the intensity of the images still shocked her.

At last the doctor left the stand, and the patrolmen who had responded to her frantic call the day of the murder testified.

Renata Hatcher took the stand, regal in a mauve suit, her eyes dramatically shadowed. Her gaze swept the courtroom, fastening on her daughter-in-law with such hatred that Laurel flinched.

"Tell us about the relationship between your son and his wife," Jackson instructed her.

"They had their differences. I heard them argue many times," Renata said calmly. "She nagged at him, trying to get him to move away and give up his position at Hatcher & Brody. She kept him stirred up and discontented. My son was very troubled by it."

"How would you describe their marriage?"

"Laurel Wilson never loved my son."

Jim rose. "Objection."

The judge nodded. "Sustained."

Laurel couldn't stop the tears from trickling down her cheeks. She bit her top lip, yearning for Dan's comforting embrace.

Jim put Renata through a scathing cross-examination, putting in doubt her assertions that Laurel had prepared to leave her husband. When Renata left the stand, Judge Hurst recessed court until the following morning.

Once the jury left the room, Laurel got shakily to her feet. Dan entered and came quickly to the defense counsel's table and put his arms around her.

"I told you not to do that," Jim said under his breath.

"Buzz off," said Dan.

Laurel chuckled against his shoulder. She knew a torrent of tears was just a breath away. "Can we leave?"

Dan squeezed her. "Is there a back way out of here?" he asked Jim.

"If you'll let go of her, I'll show you."

On their way out of the courthouse, they dodged reporters and photographers, but in the parking lot Laurel unexpectedly came face-to-face with Tina Mason.

"Tina, I'm glad to see you."

Tina faced her without smiling, a crease between her eyebrows. "Larry and I go back a long time with Bob." She looked hard at Laurel. "Renata Hatcher's had her own way for too long. You oughtn't to lose everything like that."

Laurel was surprised, and she smiled in gratitude. "Thank you for coming."

Tina turned her gaze on Dan, and Laurel felt her face flush.

"Your lawyer has Larry down as a witness," Tina said. "I suppose they'll ask him about the golf game again."

"I suppose," Laurel said.

Tina's eyes narrowed. "They're trying to connect Larry to this mess Wayne Hatcher's in about that bridge he built in New Hampshire."

"I'm sorry." Laurel swallowed hard, not sure what else to say. How much did Tina know about her husband's involvement in the bidding fraud?

"Come, Laurel, you can't discuss this," Dan said softly. She turned and walked with him to the car.

"Find anything?" Jim asked when the four of them were settled before the fireplace at the cottage.

"Maybe." Dan took out his notebook. "I think those witnesses will help us."

Jim picked up a pen and tapped it on the desktop. "Tell me."

"Well, the neighbor on the east side of Bob and Laurel's house, Mrs. Harris, says she saw Bob arrive home about 11:30 a.m., in a blue sports car. He and the driver went inside. She wasn't sure how long the guest had stayed, but that jibes with Larry Mason's story."

"I remember her," Laurel said.

"What else?" Jim leaned back in his armchair.

"The second neighbor, Frederick Wells, lives across the street. He said he saw the car in the Hatchers' driveway when he went outside after lunch, at approximately 1:15 p.m."

Jim shook his head. "That's almost two hours later. Mason didn't stay that long."

"I know, but Mr. Wells won't back down on it. He's positive of the time, and he says he told the police about it when they first came around after the murder. He said he doesn't know what Mrs. Harris saw, but it was definitely Larry Mason's car that afternoon. Larry visited Bob a lot, and Mr. Wells said he'd met him a few times. The car had a country club parking sticker in the rear window on the passenger side. Wells says he noticed it that day. And he's a retired navy commander. He'd be a credible witness."

Jim stroked his chin. "I admit I discounted that because of Mason's deposition. He took Bob home, stepped inside for a few minutes and then left. I figured one of the two neighbors had the time they saw the car wrong."

"What if they don't?" Dan asked. "This could be the ammunition we need to blow the case wide open."

Dan, Laurel and Judy sat on the dock that night eating ice cream cones. The sun dipped below the evergreens, and the plaintive cry of a loon drifted down the lake.

"Jim says it didn't go badly," Judy said, sitting down on the dock with her cherry vanilla scoop. "When we start calling our witnesses, things will look a lot better."

"That's what he told me last time." Laurel swished her bare feet in the cool water and licked her peppermint cone. *Say goodbye to all the small pleasures,* she told herself.

Dan crunched the last of his cone, then bent to rinse his hands in the lake. He wiped them on his shirttail and hitched over closer to Laurel.

Judy swatted at a mosquito. "Have you got the bug spray?"

"I think it's up in the bathroom," Laurel said.

Judy got up and went humming up the path to the cottage.

Deliberately, Laurel ate her cone, one crisp bite at a time. Dan slid his right arm around her, and she burrowed in, trying to get closer to him yet not looking at him.

He bent and put a soft kiss just below her left earlobe.

Laurel popped the tip of the cone into her mouth and crunched it, then licked her fingers.

"You want more ice cream?" Dan asked.

"No."

They sat looking out over the lake.

"The verdict won't change my feelings for you," Dan said. "Whatever God brings, we'll deal with it."

She clutched him tighter and sighed.

Strains of music came from the cottage, and Dan raised his head to listen.

"That Judy. She asked me yesterday if she could use my violin to practice the Haydn." He turned to Laurel again and rubbed his face softly against her hair and kissed her temple. "I've got to believe God will work this out and you'll go free."

She put her hand up to his cheek. "I want to believe it, too."

The music stopped, and a few minutes later, Judy came down the path. Laurel moved away from Dan and felt cold in the breeze off the lake.

Judy came onto the dock carrying Dan's phone and the bug spray. "You left this on the table, and it rang, so I answered. Mr. Hight wants to talk to you." She handed it to Dan.

"Yeah, Jim?" He sat up straighter. "When?"

Laurel held her breath.

"Okay," Dan said. "Yeah, I'll be there."

"What?" Laurel asked as he hung up.

"Jack Brody's confessed to fraud, and they've arrested Larry Mason as his accomplice."

At seven-thirty the next morning, Jim rang the doorbell at the Mason house. Tina opened the door, her eyes bloodshot and her face blotchy.

"Thank you for seeing us, Mrs. Mason," Jim said gently. "This is my investigator. May we come in?"

She stared blankly at him for a moment, then took a weary step back. Jim and Dan followed her into the family room. Dan tried not to stare, but the room demanded attention. The cathedral ceiling soared to the height of the second story, and the entire south wall was glass, overlooking a rushing stream edged by forest. If he'd ever imagined a dream house, it might have looked something like this.

"I've been up all night, Mr. Hight. What is it that's so urgent?"

Tina sat down on the cream velvet sofa, and Jim took a chair facing her. Dan went to stand with his back to the fieldstone fireplace.

"First, let me express my condolences. I heard of your husband's arrest last night. I don't wish to cause you any further grief, but this is a matter of vital importance."

Tina eyed him coldly. "Is Laurel's trial going forward?"

"Yes. We have to be in the courtroom at nine, so I won't keep you long. But you must realize there are some problems with your husband's account of the day Bob was murdered."

Tina took a deep breath. "I'm still in shock, Mr. Hight. I can't believe Larry would be involved in this bidding thing, but—" Fresh tears streamed down her cheeks, and she pulled a crumpled tissue from her pocket. "Larry said his lawyer will get him the best deal he can. This has been very difficult."

"I'm sure it has." Jim waited as she wiped her face. Dan stared out the window and wished they hadn't come. Until he remembered the danger surrounding Laurel.

"Mrs. Mason, in his deposition your husband testified that he slept most of the afternoon on the day Bob was killed."

"Yes. He came home with an awful headache. I gave him some tablets and sent him to bed."

"What did you do that afternoon?"

"Me?" Tina stared at Jim.

"Larry's car was back at the Hatchers' house around one-fifteen the day of the murder," Jim said. "If Larry didn't drive it there, who did?"

Tina sat very still, but her upper lip trembled.

Jim leaned forward. "I have to warn you, Mrs. Mason, I'm having you subpoenaed as a witness. You could be called to testify as early as this afternoon. I should have looked into it more closely before, but I assumed that one of the neighbors made an error in the time he saw the car. But the two witnesses we have in this matter are credible. I think their statements will stand up in court."

"Are you going to accuse Larry of the murder now?" Tina's voice cracked. "Because he didn't do it."

"No, I don't think he did."

She watched him, her breath shallow and fast.

"Where were you at one-fifteen that afternoon, Mrs. Mason?"

Dan stepped forward and put his hand on Jim's shoulder. Jim stood up and Dan sat down beside Tina. He looked at her for a long moment, a great sorrow weighing on his heart. "Mrs. Mason, you were a friend to Laurel. You treated her well when Bob's family rejected her. You cared about her."

"She's a decent girl." Tina reached for a fresh tissue.

"When Laurel was accused of killing Bob, you felt sorry for her."

Tina looked down at her hands. "Yes. Her in-laws treated her like dirt, and she didn't deserve it."

"Please." Dan touched her sleeve. "If Laurel is convicted, she will go to prison for a very long time. And she's innocent. You know that."

Jim moved toward him, but Dan held out one hand, and he stopped.

"I can't bear it if she goes to prison," Dan whispered. "Just the same as you can't stand it if your husband does. Please don't sacrifice her life when you know what really happened that day."

Tina drew in a ragged breath and glanced toward Jim. "You can't make me testify against myself or Larry."

Jim sat down again. "That's right. But I can give the information we've uncovered to the police and insist they reopen the investigation. In the meantime, your friend might be put in prison for a crime she didn't commit. She's already spent more than a year in jail unjustly, and it's burdened you all this time. Won't you do the right thing, Mrs. Mason?"

EIGHTEEN

Laurel sat through another day of listening to the prosecution's witnesses' testimony against her. Despite a long session in the judge's chambers, Jim was required to wait his turn to call witnesses to introduce Tina Mason's revelation.

Dan put his arm around Laurel as they entered the cottage Tuesday evening. "It's going to be all right, sweetheart."

"Jim said the judge might insist they finish the trial and let the jury deliberate."

"Let's pray," Dan said. They bowed their heads, and Dan prayed once more. Laurel held his hand and added her silent petitions.

"I'll always remember this time with you," she whispered when he had finished.

"You're not crying are you?" He leaned back so he could see her face, and her eyes were huge.

"Danny, we could still lose this. If it's bad news, you've got to go back to Ohio and don't look back. I mean it." She buried her face in his shoulder.

"Shh. That's not going to happen. God is in control."

"But you know things don't always go the way we think they should."

"Hush, now." He stroked her hair. "You're going free tomorrow."

She squeezed him tightly.

"Kiss me, Laurel."

Slowly, she lifted her face to his. He could almost read her thoughts: this could be the last time.

He bent his head to meet her, determined to kiss her so thoroughly she would never forget it. She returned his embrace with great tenderness and longing.

Dan held Laurel's hand as they walked down the hallway toward the courtroom Wednesday morning.

"Chin up," Jim said when she joined him at the defense counsel table. "I'm optimistic."

"May we sit in the family's row now?" Judy asked.

"Sure, why not?"

Dan and Judy settled into chairs behind them, and the jurors filed into their box.

"All rise," the bailiff intoned.

They stood, and Judge Hurst entered briskly from the door behind the desk. When he sat, they all sat.

Laurel's stomach roiled. She felt as though her chest were being squeezed by a giant. She took a deep breath. *Dear God, get me through this.*

She knew she might not have another chance to swim in the cool, deep lake water or sit on the dock and watch the loons glide by. To lay her head on Dan's shoulder, or kiss him again in the moonlight. Today could be her last day of freedom. The ache in her chest eased to a heavy, congested feeling. She tried to take longer, deeper breaths and calm herself.

She glanced toward the prosecutor's table. From the row behind it, Wayne and Renata Hatcher watched her malevolently.

At last Jim stood to open his case. "The defense calls Tina Mason."

Tina advanced slowly toward the witness chair. She wore rumpled slacks and a loose print blouse. Her face was haggard, and she had neglected her makeup that morning. As she sat down, she glanced toward Laurel without expression. The bailiff swore her in.

"Mrs. Mason," Jim began, "what did you do the day of the murder?"

"I went to the grocery store in the morning."

"You were at home when your husband returned after the golf game?"

"Yes."

"And what did he tell you?"

"That he had a headache. I…got him some Tylenol."

"Now, Mrs. Mason, yesterday you spoke to me, and you said that your husband told you that day that Bob Hatcher was going to the police with some information about his uncle's activities."

Tina nodded. "That's right."

Jim turned and paced back toward the table where Laurel sat. "You also told me that Larry said he could get in trouble if Bob turned in his uncle, Jack Brody, for cheating on construction bids for Hatcher & Brody."

Tina moistened her lips. "Yes."

Jim nodded. "You then told me that you were afraid.

You sent your husband to bed, and while he slept, you drove to Bob Hatcher's home to confront him. Is that true?"

"Yes." Tears glistened in Tina's eyes.

Sympathy for her friend surged through Laurel. She closed her eyes and prayed silently, *Dear Lord, help Tina. Give her strength now, and let the truth be told!*

"You admitted to me that you went to Bob's house that afternoon to try to persuade him not to turn in Jack Brody, because if he did, your husband would also be implicated in the bidding fraud."

"That's correct. Bob knew someone was helping Jack fix the bids, but he didn't know it was Larry. I begged him not to turn Jack in."

Jim walked toward her and placed his hands on the railing before the witness chair. "Now, Mrs. Mason, you are not on trial here, but you confided to me yesterday that, when you pleaded with Bob Hatcher not to reveal this situation, Bob refused to do what you asked."

"Yes, he did." She buried her face in her hands. "I just couldn't believe it. Jack apparently had talked Larry into helping him get some information from a rival builder. Larry said that if Bob told, he could…he could go to jail."

"And Bob wouldn't listen to your pleas."

"He said he had to do…what was right."

"You also told me that, in the passion of the moment, you took a handgun from the case where you knew Bob kept it, and you turned and fired it at him."

After a long pause, Tina whispered, "Yes."

Jackson jumped up, but Hurst waved his hand at him.

"No more questions," Jim said.

Laurel stared at Tina, numb to her toes.

Myron Jackson looked at Tina and sighed. "No questions."

Judge Hurst sat with the gavel in his hands, looking at Tina. "Do you have an attorney, Mrs. Mason?"

"Yes, your honor."

"All right, you may step down."

Tina stared at Laurel for a moment, tears wet on her face. The courtroom was utterly silent as she walked down the aisle and out the door, her head high, her eyes straight ahead.

The judge tapped his gavel and turned toward the jury box. "I hereby dismiss the members of the jury. Thank you for your service."

The jurors stirred and looked at each other in confusion.

Hurst turned toward the defense table. "In light of this testimony, I will exercise my right to dismiss the charges of murder against Laurel Wilson Hatcher."

A cheer broke out, and Hurst tapped his gavel. When it was quiet, he said, "Mrs. Hatcher has suffered for two years under the public perception that she murdered her husband. She spent sixteen months in the Kennebec County Jail for a crime she did not commit. For that, I am deeply sorry."

Laurel inhaled slowly, unable to take her eyes from the judge's face. Her hands trembled, and she clasped them in her lap.

Judge Hurst nodded at her. "Mrs. Hatcher, I would like to say, on behalf of the state of Maine, you are free to go, and we regret the suffering and sorrow you have endured."

Laurel smiled tearfully at him. She turned toward Jim.

He was smiling. She turned around, and Dan catapulted toward her. He hugged her close, his eyes shut.

"Thank you, Lord," he breathed in her ear.

Judy embraced her next, then Jim. Dan placed a clean handkerchief in her hand, and she swiped at her errant tears. Around them, spectators gathered their belongings to leave. Wayne and Renata Hatcher strode toward the door, Renata's face etched with bitterness.

"There will be reporters in the hallway," Jim said, and Laurel nodded. She could face the lions now without fear. Dan's tender smile encouraged her, and she squeezed his hand.

"You can speak freely now," Jim went on. "Give them a positive spin—I'm thrilled with the outcome—something simple like that." He closed his briefcase and lifted it. "Ready?"

Judy walked ahead with Jim, and Dan stayed at Laurel's side. As they left the courtroom, cameras flashed in Laurel's face.

"Mrs. Hatcher, Mrs. Hatcher!"

The press crowded around with questions.

"How do you feel about the judge's ruling?"

"Are you staying in Maine?"

"Were you surprised at Mrs. Mason's testimony?"

She pulled in a deep breath. "I'm pleased, of course, at the way things went today. I thank God for the outcome, and for my freedom."

She walked quickly with Dan down the stairs to the lobby. Jim and Judy came close behind.

"Get out of here," Jim advised. "I doubt the press will

find you, but if they do, refer them to me. I'll wrap up the paperwork and call you tomorrow morning."

They hurried to Judy's car.

"Get in the back with Dan," Judy said. Laurel started to protest, but saw several photographers headed their way. Dan opened the door, and she dove into the backseat. Judy pulled into the street and away from the crowd that had gathered in front of the courthouse.

They rolled past the county jail, and Laurel stared toward the unforgiving stone walls. Tears welled in her eyes.

"I'm so glad I'm not in there right now!"

Dan reached for her hand. "It's over," he said softly.

"You told me it would be. I should have believed you." She smiled up at him.

Dan leaned over to kiss her. "What do you want to do now?"

"Jim wants me to stay for a few days to tie up some loose ends. Do you mind being at the cottage a little longer?"

"How about it, Judy?" Dan asked.

She glanced at him in the rearview mirror as she pulled up at a stoplight.

"Stay as long as you want."

They drove back to the cottage and changed into casual clothes. Dan called his parents with the good news. Judy insisted on cooking dinner, so Dan and Laurel walked down the path to the dock. Laurel sank into a deck chair and sighed.

Dan pulled another chair close to hers and sat down. "Tired?"

"Mmm."

They sat in silence as the sun sank behind the pines. A loon called and its mate answered. Laurel could see them bobbing in the water, near the point across the cove.

She reached for Dan's hand. "I can never thank you enough."

He took a deep breath. "Laurel, we agreed to wait until the trial was over to discuss the future. I don't want to rush you…"

She rolled her head to the side and gazed into his gray eyes. "I think the right time has come."

His smile was eager and at the same time content. "You sure?"

"Yes."

He turned sober. "Can you wait just a minute? There's something I need to…" He glanced anxiously up toward the cottage.

"I'll be here."

He leaned over and kissed her, then got up. "I'll be back in thirty seconds."

Dan dashed through the kitchen, conscious of Judy's stare, and into his room. He fumbled with the dresser drawer and pulled out a small box.

"Supper in ten minutes," Judy called as he charged back through the kitchen.

Dan slowed and glanced at his watch. "We might be delayed a bit."

"What's up?" Judy opened the oven and slid in a tray of biscuits, then looked at him more closely. "What's that?"

Dan smiled. "It's, um, something I bought for Laurel." His smile was becoming a first-class clown grin.

Judy's jaw dropped. "Now? You're asking her now?"

"Well…"

Judy untied the strings of her apron. "Wait! Let me get the violin!"

"Oh, I don't know.…"

She ran for the next room. "Go! Just go slowly."

Dan went through the closed-in porch and down to the dock.

"Sorry," he told Laurel. "Judy waylaid me."

Strains of Mozart drifted over them.

"I thought she was cooking."

"She is. She's a versatile woman."

Dan knelt on the dock and took Laurel's hands in his. The moon rose behind him, sending its rays across the dark water. They looked at each other for a long moment.

"I love you so much," he whispered.

Laurel squeezed his hands. "I love you, Danny."

He nodded. "Laurel, will you marry me?"

Two tears rolled down her cheeks, but she was smiling. "Yes."

He pulled her into his arms and held her close. "I…got a ring."

She laughed. "When?"

"Last night, after you went to bed. I made a run to the mall." He sat back on his heels and held out the box. "If you don't like it…"

"Hush." She bent forward and kissed him lightly.

Dan smiled and opened the lid, revealing a sparkling diamond nested in a twined Celtic band of white gold.

Laurel caught her breath. "It's beautiful."

He reached for her left hand. "I'd be honored if you wore it." He slid the ring onto her finger. "This means I'll always love you."

She melted into his arms once more, as the music drifted over the lake.

EPILOGUE

Six months later

Laurel watched the mirror through tear-filled eyes as Judy arranged her veil. Judy caught her gaze in the glass. "Hey, there, the bride's not supposed to cry."

Laurel looked down at her ivory satin gown. "I'm just so happy. It seemed like this day would never come."

"Well, it has, and you need to go out there with a radiant smile." Judy put a tissue in her hand, and Laurel wiped her eyes.

"Did I ruin my mascara?"

Judy eyed her critically. "Nope. You look super."

The door to the room opened and Dan's sister, Becky, came in, holding up the skirt of her rose gown.

"How are you doing, almost-sister?"

Laurel smiled. She and Becky had become close friends over the past few months. "I think I'm ready."

"Great. You look wonderful." Becky kissed Laurel's cheek. "Mom and Dad are being seated. Pastor Newman is in the foyer with Donna, Marissa and the kids, and the church is full and eager."

Judy laughed. "You and Dan have a lot of friends."

"Mostly Dan's friends, but they've all been good to me."

"It's nice that your old pastor and his wife could come from Maine," Becky said.

Laurel nodded, wiping away a last tear. "I was thrilled when Pastor Newman said he'd come to give me away and take part in the ceremony."

Judy lifted Laurel's bouquet of pink and white roses from its box. "Here you go."

Laurel held out her arms. "Thanks. Aren't they beautiful?"

"Everything's perfect," Becky said. "Even the weather. I thought yesterday you'd have a terrible day. But it's sunny and warm out now."

"Are all of the musicians here?" Judy asked.

"Yep." Becky grinned. "Musicians and cops. The church is crawling with them."

Judy laughed and picked up her bouquet. "I'm glad so many of Dan's friends could come. We'll have some great music at the reception."

"We'd better get out there," Becky said. "Are you ready?"

Laurel nodded and reached to kiss Judy. "Thank you for everything, dear friend."

Judy winked at her and led the way to the door.

In the foyer, Marissa Ryan was holding Patrick's hand, and Donna Wyman, Laurel's other bridesmaid, was helping her four-year-old daughter, Reagan, decide in which hand to hold her basket of flower petals. From inside the auditorium, strains of Beethoven floated to them, and Laurel knew Judy and Dan's friends were on the job.

She stepped up to embrace Pastor Newman, and he

grinned and tucked her hand through his arm. "You look lovely, my dear."

They waited while the wedding party entered the church. Judy gave her a last smile and went down the aisle.

Laurel took a deep breath and stepped into the doorway with Pastor Newman. The size of the crowd surprised her, but she focused her attention farther away, at the end of the long aisle, where Dan stood with his three brothers and Terry Wyman. He stared at her, and his eyes held a look of such pride and joy that Laurel caught her breath. *Lord, thank You! Help me to measure up to his expectations.*

And to think she had almost turned Dan away last spring, too fearful to let him into her chaotic life. As the music cue changed and she stepped forward, she returned his smile. A flash of nervousness hit her, but Pastor Newman patted her hand, and she went on beside him with renewed courage.

God had answered her prayers, and she and Dan would have the future they had dreamed of. She'd won the civil lawsuit against her in-laws, enabling her to pay Jim Hight after all, and they had found an old brick farmhouse five miles from Dan's parents' home. Laurel had used part of the remaining money from her settlement to furnish and decorate the house. Now she was ready to start a new stage of her life. Dan had been promoted to detective, and Laurel had set up her studio in an upstairs bedroom in their new home.

She smiled at Dan as she approached the altar, and her groom's eyes gleamed with love. Life as Mrs. Dan Ryan could only be good!

* * * * *

Dear Reader,

The idea for Laurel and Dan's story came to me several years ago, but it took me some time to put it all together. I knew I wanted to write about a woman who felt she stood alone against the world, and the good man who came along to champion her cause. Dan and Laurel are tested physically, spiritually and emotionally as they seek to clear Laurel's name. Both grow as they learn to trust God and follow the leads He places in their path. Laurel almost gives up hope that she will be vindicated. Dan, Judy and Jim help her to find the strength she needs to continue the fight.

There are really two heroes in *Just Cause*. Laurel's deceased husband, Bob Hatcher, stood strong against people who wanted him to do evil. Dan supports Laurel in honoring Bob as an honest man who dies because he did right. Bob's presence is felt throughout the book. Dan and Laurel find that the best memorial for him is proving his high character.

Writing about people who need God's power in their lives and showing them grow stronger as they recognize it is a real challenge, but very satisfying. I hope it will encourage others to turn to Him.

I love to hear from readers. Contact me through my Web site, where you can e-mail me or sign up for my monthly book drawing, at www.susanpagedavis.com.

Susan Page Davis

QUESTIONS FOR DISCUSSION

1. Have you ever been accused of a crime you didn't commit? What were your feelings? Where did you turn for help and support?

2. Laurel receives permission from the court to leave her home state and use her maiden name. Are there times when you wish you could disappear and start a new life incognito? Why? What would you do instead?

3. Laurel avoids telling people about her past because she fears their reaction. At what point would you tell a new acquaintance about something painful in your past? How would you deal with rejection or misunderstanding?

4. Dan wants to take his relationship with Laurel slowly because of his past disappointment, in spite of his early feelings for her. When he learns she is widowed, he renews this resolve. How long do you think a man or woman should wait after a breakup or bereavement to start a new romantic relationship? How can rushing in be harmful?

5. What could Laurel have done for Renee when she got out of prison to keep Renee from feeling she'd broken her promise, and yet not abet her in doing more wrong?

6. Music is an important part of Dan's life. What does music add to your life, and how do you incorporate it into your daily activities?

7. Laurel feels vulnerable after her apartment is broken into twice. She and Dan take precautions to keep her and the people around her safe. What security measures do you take to safeguard yourself and those you love? Will God always protect us from physical and emotional harm?

8. When bad things happen in spite of our best precautions, how can we feel secure?

9. Laurel lost her family early, and she envies Dan his large, loving family. How can we extend the love and feelings of belonging our families have to those with no family?

10. When Laurel's trial is dismissed, the judge makes a formal apology to her from Maine. When is a public apology appropriate? Have you ever made one? How did you feel afterward?

Watch for Susan Page Davis's thrilling next novel,
WITNESS.
On sale in April 2008
from Steeple Hill Love Inspired Suspense.

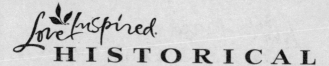

Love Inspired
HISTORICAL

INSPIRATIONAL HISTORICAL ROMANCE

Lady Bronwen of Briton was robbed of the ancestral home that was her birthright. Her only hope was a stranger—a Norman and a sworn enemy of her family. Can Bronwen put aside her antipathy and place her trust in the pure, untainted love she saw shining in this man's eyes—and follow him to a new world?

Look for

The BRITON

by

CATHERINE PALMER

Available February 12.

www.SteepleHill.com

LOOK FOR TWO NOVELS FROM THE NEW LOVE INSPIRED HISTORICAL SERIES EVERY MONTH.

Steeple Hill®

LIH82781

Love Inspired.
HISTORICAL

INSPIRATIONAL HISTORICAL ROMANCE

THE McKASLIN CLAN

Thad McKaslin never forgot Noelle, and her return to the Montana Territory rekindled his feelings for her. Will Noelle see how much Thad cares for her, or will her need for independence make her push him away?

Look for

Homespun Bride
by

JILLIAN HART

Available February 12.

LOOK FOR TWO NOVELS FROM THE NEW LOVE INSPIRED HISTORICAL SERIES EVERY MONTH.

Steeple
Hill®

www.SteepleHill.com

LIH82782

Love Inspired. SUSPENSE

RIVETING INSPIRATIONAL ROMANCE

Thanks to lies told by Leigh McAllister's family, Cole Daniels's father was wrongly imprisoned. Now that Leigh and Cole were both back in Wyoming, he was sure she held the key to clearing his father's name. But Cole's quest for justice was complicated by the escalating sabotage of Leigh's vet clinic and his growing feelings for her.

Snow Canyon Ranch:

Sinister family secrets lurk in the majestic Wyoming Rockies.

Look for

VENDETTA

by ROXANNE RUSTAND

Available February wherever books are sold.

Steeple Hill®

www.SteepleHill.com

LIS44277

Love Inspired®

SUSPENSE

RIVETING INSPIRATIONAL ROMANCE

Despite warnings to leave Magnolia campus, Lauren Owens couldn't, wouldn't—not when she'd finally found her way back to Seth Chartrand, who'd broken her heart years ago. And not when the cold-case murder remained scarily unsolved—including the young woman's identity. Because Lauren had a sinking feeling she knew exactly who the victim was...

REUNION REVELATIONS

Secrets surface when old friends—and foes—get together.

Look for

Missing Persons
by SHIRLEE McCoy

Available February wherever books are sold.

Steeple Hill®

www.SteepleHill.com

LIS44278

REQUEST YOUR FREE BOOKS!

2 FREE RIVETING INSPIRATIONAL NOVELS
PLUS 2 FREE MYSTERY GIFTS

Love Inspired®
SUSPENSE

YES! Please send me 2 FREE Love Inspired® Suspense novels and my 2 FREE mystery gifts. After receiving them, if I don't wish to receive any more books, I can return the shipping statement marked "cancel." If I don't cancel, I will receive 4 brand-new novels every month and be billed just $3.99 per book in the U.S. or $4.74 per book in Canada, plus 25¢ shipping and handling per book and applicable taxes, if any*. That's a savings of 20% off the cover price! I understand that accepting the 2 free books and gifts places me under no obligation to buy anything. I can always return a shipment and cancel at any time. Even if I never buy another book from Steeple Hill, the two free books and gifts are mine to keep forever.

123 IDN EL5H   323 IDN ELQH

Name	(PLEASE PRINT)

Address	Apt. #

City	State/Prov.	Zip/Postal Code

Signature (if under 18, a parent or guardian must sign)

Order online at www.LoveInspiredSuspense.com

Or mail to Steeple Hill Reader Service™:

IN U.S.A.: P.O. Box 1867, Buffalo, NY 14240-1867
IN CANADA: P.O. Box 609, Fort Erie, Ontario L2A 5X3

Not valid to current Love Inspired Suspense subscribers.

Want to try two free books from another series?
Call 1-800-873-8635 or visit www.morefreebooks.com

* Terms and prices subject to change without notice. NY residents add applicable sales tax. Canadian residents will be charged applicable provincial taxes and GST. This offer is limited to one order per household. All orders subject to approval. Credit or debit balances in a customer's account(s) may be offset by any other outstanding balance owed by or to the customer. Please allow 4 to 6 weeks for delivery.

Your Privacy: Steeple Hill is committed to protecting your privacy. Our Privacy Policy is available online at www.eHarlequin.com or upon request from the Reader Service. From time to time we make our lists of customers available to reputable firms who may have a product or service of interest to you. If you would prefer we not share your name and address, please check here. ☐

LISUS07

Love Inspired.
SUSPENSE

TITLES AVAILABLE NEXT MONTH

Don't miss these four stories in February

VENDETTA by Roxanne Rustand
Snow Canyon Ranch

After what the McAllisters did to his father, Cole Daniels was determined never to forgive or forget. Then Leigh McAllister landed in danger, and Cole had to decide what was stronger—his old grudge or his need to protect his new chance at love.

MISSING PERSONS by Shirlee McCoy
Reunion Revelations

Lauren Owens had her job and her faith on track, and she looked forward to tackling the mystery back at Magnolia College...until the problem turned deadly. She found herself turning to ex-boyfriend Seth Chartrand for support, for safety and love.

BAYOU CORRUPTION by Robin Caroll

All Alyssa LeBlanc wanted was to distance herself from Lagniappe, Louisiana...and from ace reporter Jackson Devereaux. But once she witnessed the attack on the sheriff, she knew she couldn't walk away. Working with Jackson, Alyssa investigated the crime—and uncovered her past.

LETHAL DECEPTION by Lynette Eason

When guerillas held Cassidy McKnight captive in the Amazon, ex-Navy SEAL turned E.R. doctor Gabe Sinclair returned to his military roots to rescue her. He thought the job was done, yet danger followed Cassidy home....

LISCNM0108